WEE KINGS

BY BRENT L. ANDERSON
COVER ART BY CHUCK GILLIES

ISBN: 1475144598
ISBN 13: 9781475144598

Cover artwork by Chuck Gillies www.chuckgilliesart.com
Edited by Rachel Starr Thomson www.rachelstarrthomson.com
Internal art by: Brent L. Anderson, Caleb Anderson, Abigail Anderson
and Faith Anderson

For more information: www.WeeThreeKings.com and look for *Wee Three Kings* on Facebook

Wee Three Kings is dedicated to my children,

Caleb, Abigail, and Faith.

Thank you for your encouragement to

"Write another chapter Dad!"

Contents

Chapter One

MADE IN CHINA

Jain sat on a stool next to a small square table packed full of paint-brushes, jars of paint, mixing cups, water jars, and rolls of paper towels. In front of him was a wheeled cart with ceramic figurines. It was just one of the many wheeled carts that would be brought before him during his twelve-hour shift at the factory. Jain hurriedly dipped his brushes in different colors of paint—red, yellow, orange, blue, and black. He picked up figure after figure and put all the colors in just the right spots. He hummed a little tune as he worked.

When he was done, the cart would be taken to the kiln to be fired. After cooling, the figurines would be boxed and shipped all over the world.

The large factory was bustling with people. Conveyor belts ran in all directions. Workers in white aprons pushed carts here and there while others sat at workbenches stacked high with things to do. The conveyor belts carried boxes and items of every shape and size. The workers were of every shape and size too: old and young, male and female, fat and thin. Along one side of the factory sat long rows of painters on stools, their painting supplies crowded on small tables. Cart pushers brought them an endless supply of carts containing items to be painted to specifications.

The one thing that made Jain stand out from the rest of the workers was his smile. There were too few smiles in this factory located deep in China's industrial district. Regardless of where Jain worked, he always brought his smile with him. He had a secret, which he had tried to share with others: he had learned to be content wherever he was, and even through the drudgery of the long shifts at the factory, he stayed content enough to smile.

Jain had dreams of being a *real* artist someday, but for now, he was content to have a job where he could at least do something he enjoyed, even if there wasn't much room for creativity. The paper work orders hung on a wire at eye level at the back of the cart. They showed how things were to be painted, whether ceramics, jewelry boxes, or small trinkets. Once he had put the first color on all the pieces, the first piece was usually dry enough to start applying the second color.

A new cart of ceramic figurines was rolled in front of Jain, and he smiled up at the cart pusher—who ignored him. Jain started to work, dipping his brushes in different colors of paint while reading the work order's instructions. As he worked, Jain kept looking back at one of the figurines on the cart in front of him, one in a set of three. There was something familiar about the little face.

"Yes! That's it!" exclaimed Jain. "You look very much like my uncle, only smaller."

Workers to Jain's left and right glanced in his direction and shook their heads. *He's talking to himself again,* they thought.

The older man to Jain's right had white hair and wrinkles, and he looked like he had a permanent frown painted on his face. Jain had tried to share his secret with the old man, the secret of being content in any situation, but unfortunately, the old man seemed more interested in being grumpy. He made it clear by the look on his face that he thought Jain was a foolish and strange young man.

"Hello, Uncle," Jain said, looking again at the little ceramic man. "Who are your two friends?" The ceramic figure made no answer—it only continued to look somber and serious. "Oh, forgive me," Jain said, bowing his head, "I did not realize I was in the presence of a great wise man."

The three Christmas figurines came as a set. This was just the first batch of proofs, pieces made as the last step in the design process to make sure there were no mistakes before sending them into mass production. Soon thousands of these little men would be shipped all over the world, arriving at stores just in time for the Christmas shopping season.

Freshly printed on the sides of the boxes traveling down a conveyor belt on the other side of the factory, printed in three different languages, were the words:

The superb artistry of these exquisite hand-painted Nativity sculptures will accent even the most eloquent home. (Wise men sold separately.) Made in China.

Jain had painted cart after cart of Nativity sets during the past week: hundreds of Marys, Josephs, babies in mangers, donkeys, sheep, and shepherds. Painting Christmas figurines made him smile even more. He loved Christmas, even though he had to celebrate somewhat in secret. His uncle (his *real* uncle) was the one who had told him of Christmas and its true meaning. But some of Jain's family did not approve of his newfound faith, and the Chinese government was even worse. Jain had to worship in secret with the other members of his church. Every time they worshiped, they risked being thrown into prison.

"I will give you a little mustache and a pointy little beard—there—now you look just like my uncle," Jain said, smiling.

"Jain!" the supervisor yelled from behind. He had thick, black-rimmed glasses and smiled even less than the old man who worked next to Jain.

"Yes, sir?" Jain answered.

"The facial hair on that figure is all wrong!" bellowed the supervisor.

"Yes, sir, I just thought…"

"You don't think! You follow the work order! You don't need to think!" yelled the supervisor.

"Yes, sir. I…I…"

"You waste time! You waste paint, and you waste my patience! Now get back to work. And follow the work order!" The supervisor was already walking away before Jain could try to say anything else.

Jain looked back at the figurine, which was now sporting a little black goatee. The work order called for dark brown beards on two of the figurines, but the one that looked like his uncle was not supposed to have any facial hair.

"Well, Uncle, I think you look very handsome. Pay no attention to him. In fact, I pray a special blessing upon you and your two friends.

I pray that you will bring joy to whoever owns you, and that through you, people will remember the true meaning of Christmas."

Jain set the figure back down next to the other two wise men.

A cart pusher approached Jain's workbench very briskly. "Are these ready to go?" he asked impatiently.

"Yes, they are ready."

The cart was whisked away.

"Good-bye, Uncle." Jain waved as the cart moved away from him.

"Uncle? Is he talking to me? Is that my name?" asked the little ceramic figure with the black goatee.

"I wonder what my name is?" echoed the other two wise men.

Chapter Two

KING'S ROAD

No one noticed the chatter coming from atop the cart being wheeled across the factory floor. The cart passed through a doorway, rattled down a hall, and bumped through metal double doors. The doors swung wide, allowing a sudden burst of hot air to escape from the firing room. A large industrial kiln filled the length of the long, cement-walled room. Its steel body encased the oven bricks, forming a tunnel through which the mesh wire belt pulled objects deep into the belly of the monster oven. This was where the final step of baking the paint onto the ceramics happened.

The very moment Jain had prayed a special blessing upon the ceramic wise men, something strange—something magical—had happened. The little ceramic figurines could suddenly hear, see, think, and talk. Well, at least, they could talk to each other. The cart pusher, who was quietly whistling a tune to himself, didn't seem to hear them, even with the reduced noise in the firing room.

"Maybe if we speak louder, he will hear us," said the wise man dressed in a Middle Eastern robe and turban. His robe was painted to look like coarse linen.

"Hey you, big fella!" yelled Uncle, whose clothing was painted to look like oriental silk.

"Maybe he *can* hear us. Maybe he's just rude," said the wise man painted to look distinctly African.

"If only I could move, maybe I could get his attention," said Uncle with frustration. A shadow passed over them, and giant hands attached to unseen men picked them up and moved them from the cart. As the three wise men were swooped from the cart, they caught a glimpse of the imposing room. The firing room was not as well lit as the rest of the factory, and it was quiet, except for the steady hiss of gas that fed the fires of the kiln. The pores of the concrete walls and floor were stained with brown soot that remained even after a good scrubbing.

The wise men had been birthed into the bright, sterile environment of the factory, and now, just moments later, they found themselves in a dreary, dungeon-like room with grabbing hands and the menacing hiss of fire. They weren't at all sure they liked the change.

The cotton-gloved hands that had grabbed them set them down on a wire-mesh conveyer belt that led directly into the long furnace.

The three wise men faced the hungry, glowing mouth of the kiln. They moved slowly toward the waves of intense heat that billowed out of the oven like the hot breath of a Chinese dragon.

"Ahhh! We're going to die!" the ceramic men yelled in unison. The belt squeaked and whirred beneath them. Closer and closer to the kiln they moved.

"Wait, are we going to die? Are we even *alive?*" the African asked, right before they reached the opening. The other two stopped screaming to ponder that very logical question.

Into the kiln they went, and then everything became quiet.

LONDON, ENGLAND, THREE WEEKS LATER…

Mr. Clemons carefully unpacked the small, colorful boxes from the larger cardboard box. Foam peanuts spilled out onto the floor and stuck to anything that contained the slightest bit of static.

The shop owner peered over his reading glasses as he talked to himself. "Let's see here: we've got the salt and pepper shakers, the teacups, one box of Christmas tree ornaments, the three wise men set, and…" Puzzled, Mr. Clemons dug around in the foam. "Where is the Nativity set I ordered? It should be here."

It wasn't long before the three little ceramic figurines were unpacked with the rest of the new items. Christmas was only three months away, so Mr. Clemons was already busy putting up Christmas decorations and stocking his shelves with gift items.

"Well, hello, Sam. Where have you been hiding all day?" Mr. Clemons looked down at the fluffy, gray-and-white cat rubbing against his leg. Sam was as much a part of Clemons's General Store and Antique Shop as Mr. Clemons himself was. Their regular customers enjoyed Sam's leg rubbing and affection seeking as much as they enjoyed conversations with the cordial, gray-haired shop owner.

Clem's Store, as his regular customers and friends called it, was one of the more than one hundred and twenty shops along King's Road in London, England. Various dealers offered specialized merchandise such as antiques, period jewelry, porcelain, silver, first-edition books, boxes, clocks, prints and paintings, and the occasional piece of antique furniture. But as far as Mr. Clemons knew, Sam was the only cat employed in all of King's Road.

Mr. Clemons's wide collection included antiques, but also a wide variety of new specialty items. He had planned to display the ceramic Nativity set in the front window. He'd even bought the three wise men and the barnyard animals, which were sold separately. Thus, he was understandably frustrated to discover that the Nativity set had not come in this shipment. All he had received were the three wise men.

"Yes, yes I understand that they have been put on back order, but I don't understand why I wasn't told this when I made the order. Okay... okay, I understand," Mr. Clemons said cordially, smiling into the phone. "But what good are the wise men and their gifts if they don't have anyone to give their gifts to? Well, thank you for your help anyway." With a sigh, he placed the old-fashioned phone back on its cradle. Sam jumped up on the counter between the phone and the antique cash register and weaved his way beneath Mr. Clemons's hand.

"Well, Sam, it looks like they had a problem at the factory, and the Nativity set is on back order for the time being." Mr. Clemons stroked Sam's fur obligingly, and the cat purred his pleasure.

Jingle-ling. The bells above Mr. Clemons's door shook as a tall, lean man came through the doorway. He was dressed plainly, and he would have given a prudish impression if not for his friendly face. His neatly combed brown hair was parted on the side; bushy eyebrows crowned thoughtful eyes, and he had wrinkles formed from over fifty years of smiling.

"Hello, Mr. Clemons, and hello there, Sam—how are you on this fine day?"

"Father Andrew, what a pleasant surprise! Things are fine here." Mr. Clemons stretched his hand out and gave the priest a warm handshake. "Come in, come in. What can I help you with?"

"Well, Clem, my friend—I'm doing a little window shopping, and I'm also making sure to remind the wonderful people of King's Road that the orphanage is having its annual fundraiser very soon."

Mr. Clemons and Father Andrew gravitated toward one of the antique couches on display in the middle of the store. It wasn't too long before they were catching up with each other over cups of hot, fresh-brewed Earl Grey tea.

Jingle-ling. A girl of seventeen or eighteen stepped through the door. She was wearing a bright, cheery dress with white flowered lace that danced just below her knees and a white cardigan to ward off the late-September chill. A yellow ribbon accented the yellow, wide-brimmed hat that was a perfect match for the rose floral pattern on her yellow dress. She smiled when she saw Sam lying next to the cash register. He picked up his head and meowed a greeting.

"Oh, you're a real kitty! For a moment I thought you were stuffed."

Mr. Clemons excused himself to greet the young woman. "Sam *is* stuffed, but that's just because he eats too much and exercises too little. May I help you find something, Miss?"

"I saw the Christmas decorations in the window and had to come in and check out your store. You do realize it's only September 24th, don't you?" the young woman said.

Mr. Clemons smiled and scratched Sam behind the ears. "Well, I do love Christmas."

"Oh, I do too; Christmas is my favorite time of the year." The girl used her finger to brush a flyaway strand of sandy brown hair from her face and tuck it behind her ear. She glanced over Mr. Clemons's shoulder, and her eyes sparked with recognition.

"Father Andrew, is that you? I didn't see you sitting back there."

"Hello, Elizabeth! I almost didn't recognize you with that hat on. What a pleasant surprise." Father Andrew carried his tea with him to the front of the store. "I see you are back from your missions trip. Please, tell me all about Uganda!"

"Africa?" Clem asked with a raised eyebrow. He looked at the young lady with new interest, and Father Andrew laughed. He introduced Elizabeth and Clem, then explained how she had been volunteering at the London orphanage all through high school. She had graduated in the spring and participated in an exchange program with an orphanage in Uganda during the summer.

In return, Elizabeth got to hear the story of how Father Andrew and Clem had met and been friends for years. Soon they were all seated on the antique furniture, listening to stories of Elizabeth's Uganda experience and sipping tea.

"The orphanage was so crowded with kids. Our London orphanage stays full, but nothing like the one where we worked. Many of the rooms had cots arranged wall to wall, and some of the children had to sleep on blankets laid on the floor, but at least that was better than the streets where many of them had been living."

The men's attentive posture encouraged her to keep talking, and her passion only seemed to grow the more she talked.

"They really enjoyed listening to us read. When we realized that some of them didn't understand English very well, some of the volunteers from an American church group started acting out the stories in a kind of theatrical, slapstick version of charades."

Elizabeth chuckled. "Oh, how the children laughed! Whether they understood the story or not, it was a grand sight to see: all of those rows and rows of children laughing. Hiram he was the funniest and most animated of them all. The children all loved him!"

Father Andrew took a sip of his tea, peeked over his teacup, and shot a glancing smile at Clem when Elizabeth wasn't looking.

"It was a wonderful time," she finished. "But oh, Father Andrew, there is so much more to be done there—I only wish I could help more."

"What did you say this young man's name was—the one you met in Uganda?" Father Andrew asked in a tone that reminded Elizabeth of her dad when he was prying a little too deeply into her personal life.

"His name was…um, *is*…Hiram." Elizabeth blushed slightly, and her eyes roved the room. She set her teacup down and walked over to a shelf that was crowded with the things Mr. Clemons planned to put in the new front-window display. The bottom shelf was stuffed with fake greenery and a bag of fluffy fake snow. The middle shelves were crowded with porcelain snowmen, antique Christmas dolls, serving dishes and platters with holly painted around the edges, and saltshakers in the shape of reindeer, snowmen, Santas, and little Christmas trees. The ceramic wise men sat on the top shelf with boxes of colorful ornaments crowded around them.

"I just love the detail on these wise men," she said. "They almost look like they could talk to you."

Clem winked at Father Andrew and whispered, "You've flustered the poor girl."

"What was that?" Elizabeth called from across the room.

"Aaah, I say I'm flustered that the rest of the shipment hasn't arrived. I am waiting on the whole Nativity set—it's on back order from the factory," said Mr. Clemons. He smiled. "They're an all-new design. The first sets are just being released."

Elizabeth examined the figure in her hand. Its oriental face was thin and serious, and it had a thin black goatee. Its robe was painted smooth like silk and had a colorful Chinese design painted in greens and purples.

She picked up the next wise man. His cheeks were round, and Elizabeth thought he had a friendly, jovial face. The Middle Eastern turban, sandy robe, and dark brown beard with no mustache made him look as though he would be right at home in the desert. He was molded together with a camel, which was lying down behind him with its legs tucked under its body.

She picked up the final figure. His full, curly beard hid any discernible expression. His skin was dark, and his clothing was a distinctly African mix of brown, yellow, orange, gold, and black.

"This one looks like he could be from Uganda. When will you get the whole Nativity set?" she asked, looking back at Mr. Clemons.

"They said two to three weeks," Mr. Clemons answered.

"I'd love to see the whole set when it comes in."

Mr. Clemons rubbed the back of his neck with his hand. "Well, I plan to make it the centerpiece of my window display, so I hope it comes soon."

Elizabeth reminded Father Andrew about the Nativity scene at the orphanage. It was getting old and worn from so many years of use. She explained to Mr. Clemons how the wise men had mysteriously disappeared last year, and no one could find them anywhere.

"I fear that someone may have accidentally thrown them away when the storage closet was cleaned the previous summer." Father Andrew placed his teacup carefully on the antique side table. "They were in an old box; it would have been an easy mistake to make."

"Maybe when the whole set gets here, we could think about replacing the one at the orphanage," Elizabeth hinted.

Father Andrew picked up one of the figurines and looked at the price tag.

"Well, if that is the price of *just* the wise men, maybe my good old friend Clem would be more interested in donating them to the orphanage!"

They all laughed.

The wise men were put on display in the window for the next few months. The back-ordered Nativity set never did arrive.

More importantly, the magic that caused the wise men to talk didn't return until December 12th, just as the clock struck midnight.

Chapter Three

WHO ARE WE?

Months pass quickly, especially when you are a ceramic figurine and thus unaware of the passage of time.

The three wise men spent their holiday season as part of a festive Christmas display in the front window at Clemons's Store. The factory refunded Mr. Clemons's money when it became clear that the rest of the order would not come. Disappointed, he improvised by arranging a beautiful miniature merry-go-round as the centerpiece of his window display. Above it hung a hand-painted sign that read, "Spread the Merry Around this Christmas Season!"

The handmade merry-go-round was a full two feet wide. It plugged into the wall and lit up the window like a miniature carnival. The horses were brightly painted and went up and down, just like the real thing. The wise men stood off to the side next to an artificial Christmas tree. They were part of a large montage of all things Christmas, including porcelain snowmen, antique dolls, ornaments, a vintage Santa, fake snow, and greenery.

The shop was dark. A cuckoo clock ticked on the wall and slowly began to chirp midnight.

"That's a good question…*are* we alive?" asked the figurine with the thin black goatee.

"Wait a minute. Where are we?" asked the plump Middle Eastern figurine. "Where's the kiln? I was terrified!"

"It would appear that we are in a new place," said the figurine with the dark curly hair and beard.

They all paused to take in the scene before them. They were facing the street, which lay just on the other side of the large glass display window. The slick pavement was illuminated by streetlights and the headlights of the occasional passing car. Little else could be seen in the darkness. After a few minutes of gazing out the window, the dark, curly-haired figurine in the African robe spoke again.

"To answer the first question—are we alive? It seems that the very act of asking such a question would make the answer obvious. We are thinking, we are communicating, and therefore we are alive. As for where we are—that I do not know. But more importantly, I would present the question, *who* are we?"

This question led to a lengthy conversation, one full of guessing, supposing, and wondering. By the time the morning light started to peek through the window, the three figurines had concluded several things.

They *were* alive. Although they could not move, walk, run, or even blink, they must be alive, for they could think, see, hear, and talk. They also deduced that whatever had caused them to have life had also given them a basic knowledge of things. Deeper than that, they realized they had the wisdom to question the *what*s, the *why*s, and the *how*s of their surroundings.

For instance, they knew that a chair was a chair and that it was dark outside. They knew that the darkness was called night and that the coming light was called day. They knew that the window was made of glass and that the window was different from a door. They knew that outside of the window there was a street, a sidewalk, and a streetlight. They knew all manner of things; but how or why they knew anything at all was a mystery to them.

They decided that the one with the goatee should be called "Uncle" because they remembered hearing someone call him that when they were at the factory.

Was the person who had painted them and spoken to them so lovingly their creator? Why had they been put into the fire? Was there something more to their lives before the factory? Were there things they could not remember? All of these questions went unanswered.

Mr. Clemons arrived at 8:00 a.m. as usual. His breath could be seen in the cold air as he searched his pocket for the store keys. Sam was already pacing at the front door impatiently, waiting for Mr. Clemons to come in and fill his bowl with food, as he did every morning.

Jingle-ling. The door opened, and Mr. Clemons began his morning routine. The store didn't open for business until nine, so the shop owner had time to prepare for the day, which included bookwork, straightening and dusting, and of course, filling Sam's food bowl. Then he poured himself a cup of hot Earl Grey tea.

"It's no use," said Uncle. "We've screamed as loudly as we can. He's walked by us several times and hasn't so much as looked at us."

"Well, the *cat* looked at us—did you see him? And I'm very concerned that he had a hungry look in his eyes. He might just decide to eat us!" said the wise man figurine who looked like a plump little Arab.

The African wise man spoke solemnly. "I don't think we have anything to fear from that cat, but I do fear that our existence may be purposeless and useless. We are trapped in bodies that do not move. We can think and reason, but our voices cannot be heard. I fear that such a dismal existence can only mean one thing. We are being punished for some past wrongs, *of which we cannot even remember.*"

There was a momentary silence while the other two pondered the African's words. "If we did something wrong and are being punished, then why do we not remember it?" asked Uncle.

"That doesn't make any sense," added the Arab.

The African was unperturbed by their protests. "It makes perfect sense. If we have done something terrible and have been stuck here in these bodies as punishment, we might become content by saying, 'Well, we deserve what we have become.' But because we don't know who we are or why we are here, the punishment is even worse because we don't have the satisfaction that comes from knowing that we deserve our fate."

Uncle was not at all convinced. "That's the most ridiculous thing I have ever heard…not that I have heard a lot. I refuse to believe such an unfounded bunch of supposing, assuming, conjectural rubbish."

The three wise men didn't do much talking the rest of the day. They watched Sam warily as the cat moved about the shop, casting them a suspicious glance every now and again. The question of what their purpose in life could possibly be consumed their thoughts as they watched people scurrying up and down the busy sidewalks while an endless stream of cars and double-decker buses passed by on the street. Time after time, the *jingle-ling* of the door alerted them to the entrance of another shopper. Several people even took the time to look at the three wise men—but who wants to buy wise men that are so unique they don't match any Nativity set but one, one that is missing?

By the end of the day, even Uncle feared that maybe it *was* true—maybe they were being punished for some past wrong that none of them could remember. The plump Arab fretted all day, but he desperately wanted to be optimistic.

Oh, I really hope I'm not a bad person…but I guess if I am, I'm glad I don't know that I'm a bad person. He smiled bravely to himself. He was glad he could think of something positive. The daylight faded into dusk, and then darkness.

Chapter Four

NOT A CREATURE WAS STIRRING, EXCEPT...

The three wise men stared out the window in silence. In the background, the cuckoo clock sounded three times: *cuckoo-cuckoo...cuckoo-cuckoo...cuckoo-cuckoo.* Outside, the streetlights cast eerie shadows, and the car traffic had slowed to an occasional flash of headlights past the front of the store.

Suddenly, Uncle was startled by a noise. If he could have moved his head, he would have whipped it around to see what was making the sound.

"Did you hear that?" he said, breaking the hours of silence that had befallen them.

"Hear what?" asked the Arab.

"Look, there is a reflection in the window," said the African.

In the reflection, the wise men could see into the back of the store where two shadowy figures were lurking. As they watched, the figures began slowly moving around.

"Maybe they are the cleaning crew," whispered the Arab.

"Robbers!" said Uncle in a hushed yell.

The African couldn't resist. "Technically, if there is no one present, they would be considered burglars, not robbers, you see, because *robbery* is a crime against persons, whereas *burglary* is…"

"Oh, shut up, will you?" snapped Uncle. In the same breath, he paused and said, "How in the heck do you know that, anyway?"

"Shh! Shh! Shh!" insisted the Arab. "I think they can hear us."

Indeed, the two men in the shadows were squinting their eyes and straining their ears as if they heard something—maybe even voices.

"Meow!" Sam came out of hiding to greet the strangers.

"Hey, Nick, it's just a stupid cat," said Eddie, who was the taller of the two burglars at six foot three.

Nick may have been shorter than Eddie, but his broad shoulders, muscular chest, and square jaw made him seem bigger than his five-foot-ten frame. He had discovered weightlifting as a hobby during his time behind bars, and his physique showed it.

He was also the smarter of the two, and he had no problem flaunting that fact to his accomplice. Eddie might have added some comic relief to Nick's grim existence if he didn't find him so annoying. As far as burglars went, Eddie acted more like a clichéd bumbler out of a cartoon than a career criminal like Nick.

Even so, Nick's choice of partners was no accident. Eddie took orders and insults well, and he made the perfect fall guy if they did happen to have a run-in with the authorities. Nick would cut a deal and sell Eddie out in a heartbeat. The first thought Nick had ever had about Eddie was that he was expendable—nothing more than cannon fodder, and his attitude had not changed much since then.

"Okay, let's get busy. Remember, we're looking for the good stuff—no takin' something just cuz you think you can get a few bucks for it at a pawn shop. Look for the antique jewelry and the other stuff I told you about. I have buyers who will pay *real* money for the right items."

Nick pointed Eddie to the front of the store, and his companion moved slowly, looking around. He acted more like a person perusing a garage sale than a burglar. He stopped to look at some antique toys, picking up a tin tractor and spinning its wheels with curiosity.

Nick came up behind Eddie and smacked him in the back of the head.

"Focus! Look for the antiques that I showed you pictures of. Quit gawking at this junk as if you think you're going to discover some hidden treasure. I'm the expert!"

Back at the display window, Uncle and the African had digressed into an argument and almost forgotten about the trespassers.

"I'm sick and tired of your negativity. Why don't you take some lessons from our camel-herding friend here and look for the positive in our situation?" Uncle said.

"I don't appreciate your tone of superiority," the African said before the Arab cut him off.

"Hey!" the Arab insisted.

"What?" Uncle and the African exclaimed together as their heads spun to look at the plump, turban-wearing wise man.

"I...um... can't remember what I was going to say because...your heads just moved!" The Arab's face showed his amazement.

Uncle moved his head from side to side. "I can move my head! And I feel something else, too—I think my finger just wiggled."

The African moved his head from side to side, and then he looked back at the Arabian wise man. "Oh, great!" he exclaimed.

"What's wrong?" said Uncle.

"There goes his camel."

They watched as the camel stood up, scampered to the end of the window ledge, and jumped into the darkness.

The Arab looked at the other two, confused. "I have a camel?"

"More accurately, you *had* a camel," the African corrected. "He was right behind you. You've been leaning against him this whole time!"

The Arab smiled as he turned his head around as far as it would go. "I have a camel! I am so happy I have a camel. I wonder why he never said anything to me."

"Everyone knows that camels don't talk." The African said as he rolled his eyes.

"Hey! You just rolled your eyes; that's great!" said Uncle. "I think I can move my arms now too." Uncle moved his arms away from his body slowly and cautiously at first, as though he couldn't believe he was doing it, and the other two did the same. It was like they had been frozen, and now they were thawing from the head down. Each new movement was followed by excited chatter among them.

After a moment, Uncle and the African fell quiet and stopped moving. They looked up and past the Arab, who was waving his arms up and down and laughing.

The Arab stopped waving his arms when he realized the other two were looking at something behind him with a curious expression on their faces. "What is it?" he asked. "Did my camel come back?"

"Shh," said Uncle.

Eddie was just a few steps away. He had heard something and had seen the three little figurines moving. Before the wise men could react, he reached down and picked up the Arab. "Little battery-operated figurines like you little blokes must be worth something," he muttered.

Uncle tried not to let his lips move as he whispered to the other two wise men. "As soon as we can move our legs, we need to run and find a place to hide."

Eddie turned the Arab upside down, looking for the on/off button. He shook the little man, and then beat him against the palm of his hand.

The poor little wise man couldn't take it anymore. He let out a scream. "Put me down, you big oaf!"

Startled, Eddie dropped the figurine back onto the window ledge.

Nick yelled at Eddie, his voice carrying from the back of the store. "What's with all the racket up there? Why don't you just wave your arms while you're standing there in front of that big window so the coppers can see you when they drive by?"

"Hey, Nick, these little guys talk," Eddie said.

Eddie turned back to the figurines just in time to see the three six-inch wise men run to the end of the window ledge and start climbing down.

"Aah, come back here, you barmy little…!" Eddie reached out and grabbed the Arab before he was able to escape to the floor.

Nick appeared from the shadows, his face red with anger.

"What did you call me?" Nick asked.

Eddie started stammering. "No, no, no I was talking to this little…"

Nick shouted over Eddie as he moved closer.

"I told you to stop your gawking and get to work!"

"AHHHH!" Eddie let out a painful scream as he looked down to see a large rat—no, a miniature camel!—biting his ankle. Just then, the little Arab bit Eddie's finger.

"AHHHH! I'm being attacked!" Eddie dropped the figure and tried to kick at the camel.

Nick grabbed Eddie by the shoulder and smacked him across the face with his free hand. "Get over here!" Nick said, pulling him away from the window. "If you don't quiet down, you're going to get us both put behind bars! Now quit messing around!"

"But, but…"

Nick put his hand up to Eddie's mouth. "Not another word out of you, Eddie. Now come on, the antiques are back here." He spoke slowly and carefully this time, making sure Eddie took him seriously.

Eddie wasn't sure what had just happened. He figured it was best to do what Nick said since he couldn't explain it anyway.

Nick and Eddie quietly went to work stuffing sacks with antique jewelry, old coins, and other valuables. Not even a minute had passed when Nick suddenly froze.

"Did you hear that?" Nick whispered.

He heard the faint sound of voices, as though a phone had been knocked off the receiver and someone was still talking on the other end.

Eddie strained his ears.

"Nice kitty, nice kitty…you're a big *friendly* kitty, aren't you?" the voices said.

Nick squinted into the dark shadows. The sound appeared to be coming from somewhere near the cash register in the middle of the store. Then something caught his eye. A small, furry animal galloped out from under the table, and the gray-and-white cat chased right behind it.

Nick looked at Eddie. "Was that a rat?"

Eddie hesitated and shook his head. "Nope, it's a camel—I think it belongs to the little men," he whispered.

Nick raised his hand to slap Eddie again, but first he looked to see where Eddie was pointing his finger.

Out from under the same table came one—two—three little men, yelling, "Run, camel, run!"

Stunned, Nick looked back at Eddie.

"Told you so," Eddie said.

Chapter Five

ANGELS HEARD ON HIGH

Nick couldn't trust what his eyes were telling him. The camel and the little men were not like any remote-control devices or windup toys he had ever seen. The camel had actually *galloped*, and the little men moved like real people, only in miniature. Still, his mind searched for a rational explanation—they couldn't be what they appeared to be!

But if they were…

"Come on," he said to Eddie, tiptoeing in the direction the little men had run. Nick and Eddie zigzagged through the store and peeked around corners. There, in front of a glass cabinet full of antique dolls, was a small camel wrestling with a cat while three little men in robes looked on. The cat pinned the camel with one paw, then began licking it.

"Oh, look! They're just playing; they are friends," said the Arabian wise man.

"Well, isn't that nice," the African said flatly.

Uncle turned around quickly and scanned the room, but saw no one. "Where did the intruders go? We'd better hide."

The three moved back toward the center of the store with Uncle in the lead. There were more places to hide around all of the antique furniture, wooden chests, and shelves. After another moment's licking, the cat let the camel up, and he started to follow as well.

"Not so fast!" Nick said, appearing suddenly out of the shadows. The startled wise men looked up just in time to see a large wicker basket coming straight down over their heads.

"I got them!" Nick said. "Grab that camel; it's getting away!" But it was too late. The camel and the cat slipped through a tight space and into the darkness.

"See, I wasn't goofin' around! They are real," Eddie babbled. "What are we going to do with them, Nick?"

"I don't know—I don't even know what they are. But I bet we can find someone who will pay us a pretty penny for them." Nick turned and sat on the basket. "We need a box or something to put them in. Go look for one back there where we broke in, and keep an eye out for the camel. I'll sit here and try to figure out a plan."

Eddie followed Nick's command. At first, he moved quickly, but he slowed down as he peered into the shadows, wondering what kind of a creepy store this was. What else in the store was alive and watching his every move?

Near the storage in the back, he spied a big cardboard box. Startling him, the cat jumped about three feet up to the top of a wooden bookshelf and vanished.

Eddie shuddered. The bookshelf was in a cluttered corner and had books stacked around and on top of it. He moved slowly to the shelf and peered between two columns of stacked books where he had seen the cat disappear. From the dark passage, the small head of a camel peered back at him, moving its mouth as if it was chewing cud.

Kersplat! The camel let go with an awfully big wad of spit for such a little animal.

"Right in my eyes!" Eddie howled.

The crook pulled up the bottom half of his loose-fitting shirt and vigorously wiped his face, mumbling in disgust. As he was wiping his eyes, for a brief moment he thought he saw a bright light, as if the lights in the store had come on. But when he moved his shirt away from his face, it was still dark—and the camel was gone.

"Hey, Nick, I found the camel—and he spit on me!"

Silence answered.

"Nick," Eddie repeated. "Nick? Nick, did you hear me?"

Eddie fidgeted in the eerie silence.

Smoothing his damp shirt back into position, Eddie walked over to the cardboard box. "And this is my favorite shirt. I hope it doesn't stain." He shook his head. It was way too creepy in here.

Eddie grabbed the box and headed back to where he had left Nick sitting on the basket.

Nick wasn't sitting on the basket when Eddie got there. The basket was turned upright, and the little men were nowhere to be seen.

"Nick, Nick? Where did you go?"

Eddie was really getting nervous now. Something in the air had changed. It was as if there was an unseen presence, as if something was watching him with a heavy gaze.

"Nick, come on; this ain't funny."

Eddie slowly turned the corner and looked down a long aisle. There was Nick, sitting with his back against the wall and his knees pulled up close to his chest. But what Eddie noticed when he looked at him was strange and uncharacteristic for his rough and tough accomplice: Nick's face was white. He looked like a terrified little boy who desperately wanted to hide but had been caught and could only shrink into the corner, paralyzed with fear.

Now Eddie was starting to feel panicked. Nick didn't joke around like this. As a matter of fact, Nick never joked around at all. Nor had Eddie ever seen Nick show fear. He had seen Nick in situations with guns pulled on him, in run-ins with the police, and in all sorts of other jams, but Nick was always cocky, and he always kept his cool.

He wasn't keeping his cool right now.

"Hey, Nick, w-w-what's going on?" Eddie asked, his eyes darting from side to side.

Nick didn't answer.

"Are you hurt? Here, let me help you up." Eddie walked toward him with an outstretched hand.

Instead of reaching out to meet Eddie's hand, Nick pulled his knees in tighter. He was trembling. He shook his head *no* like a nervous Chihuahua.

Eddie froze as light flooded the room from behind him. He looked Nick in the eyes. "Cops?" he whispered.

Another nervous shake of the head from Nick.

Eddie took a deep gulp. Slowly, he put his hands up in the classic surrender position, then turned around.

There, facing him, was a large, muscular man with long, flowing hair. The man was taller than Eddie with a stern face that might have been carved out of stone. His eyes pierced right into Eddie's heart.

Eddie now understood why Nick looked the way he did. Eddie couldn't move, either; he couldn't swallow; he couldn't even look away. Eddie felt deep in his soul that this was *it*—he was about to die. This man was going to destroy him. At the same time, he was also struggling to figure out who this man was…no, *what* this man was.

The stranger's eyes were truly piercing. They glowed like jewels in a display case with a light shining behind them. Eddie realized, suddenly, that the glow lighting up the room was not from a spotlight or the store lights, but from the man. The light did not come just from his eyes, either—his entire body was luminescent: his face, his hair, his full-length robe, the sword on his hip, and his wings…he had wings!

The word *wings* echoed in Eddie's mind. Yes, he was about to die. He collapsed to the floor. There was no use saying anything. He knew he could not run or hide, so he dropped in anticipation of the inevitable. His life started flashing before his eyes: all the mistakes and bad things he had ever done; all the chances he'd had to change, to take a different path, and to become a better person. All the choices he'd made raced through his mind, convicting him on every level of his existence: stolen cars, broken promises, lying, cheating, laughing at the misery of others, stealing from his own grandmother…the images came, drowning him in a flood of his life's choices.

"Look at me," echoed the voice of Death.

Eddie hesitated, and then looked up at the angel.

"The Lord is not very happy with you, Eddie," the angel said.

Eddie dropped his gaze to the floor.

"Look at me," the angel commanded again.

Eddie looked up.

"You will not die this night. No man knows the day or the hour of his own death. It may be tomorrow, it may be next week or next year, but it will not be this night."

Eddie knew he could believe what he was hearing, and the angel's words broke the edge off his fear just enough that he could speak. "Wh-wh-what do you want with me?" Eddie stuttered.

"I have already talked to Nick. Now I will talk to *you.*" The angel's voice was steady and strong. Eddie hoped for some fluctuation in tone that might indicate the angel was softening a little or feeling some sort of pity for him, but it did not happen.

"You know who you have been, the things you have done, the chances the Lord has given you to turn to him and be saved—but you have followed your own selfishness instead of following the Lord."

Ashamed and trembling, Eddie said, "It's true."

"Come to the Lord and be saved," the angel commanded.

Eddie's voice trembled and cracked. "How? I...I don't know what to do."

The angel's voice showed no pity, but there was a hint of increased urgency in his tone. "Believe. The Lord will do the rest. Knock and the door will be opened to you. Seek him and you will find him. Choose this day the gift, or choose this day the curse. And do not think to yourself that this vision alone will save you! You are not the first men to receive a sign such as this. And yet, when the fear and trembling have passed, some men still return to their old ways."

"I want to—I want to do what is right," Eddie said.

"Go then, and seek the Lord. Both of you."

Nick and Eddie remained frozen in fear.

"Go NOW!" the angel boomed, pointing to the back of the store where the criminals had broken in.

Nick and Eddie did not dare stay frozen and risk making the angel repeat himself. Fear had paralyzed them, but an even deeper, more powerful fear got them moving again.

Nick and Eddie moved slowly at first, then more quickly as they neared the back of the store. When they entered the alley, they burst into an all-out run to their car, which they had parked two blocks away. They jumped in, breathing heavily, and sat there staring straight ahead, their breath fogging up the windows. They didn't speak. They didn't look at each other. They just sat there, minds racing. All they could hear was the rhythmic sound of their heartbeat pounding in their ears. Nick finally started the car, and they drove off in silence.

Chapter Six

NEW NAME, NEW HOME

The angel of the Lord turned to the three wise men and the camel, all of whom had been standing in the shadows watching.

"The Lord has a plan and a purpose for you. You must have no more talk of being useless or having no purpose."

Moving into the open aisle, the three wise men smiled and nodded their heads, with the camel sneaking a smug look at the African. The angel did not have to explain everything to them, at least not in words. They seemed to gain knowledge just by being in his presence.

"First, your names: the Lord has names for each of you."

The angel looked at Uncle first. "You have already been named. A servant of the Lord thought you reminded him of his uncle, and your name shall remain *Uncle.* Let your name be a reminder that people are made in the image of God, just as the three of you are made in the image of man."

The angel looked at the African.

"You are a serious one, and you shall be called *Harold*. Harold is a serious name. But do not allow your solemnity to get in the way of your purpose, or you may be led astray by cynical thinking."

Harold nodded in understanding, but the angel was not finished.

"There is a song that people sing this time of year which has the words, 'Hark, the herald angels sing.' Remember that I, the angel of the Lord, have given you your name. When you become too serious or too proud, remember that your very name is a play on words. This is so that you might remain humble."

The angel nodded to the Arab and said, "Look at your robe."

The Arab looked down to his right side, near his foot. A piece of his robe was missing. In his present form, it appeared to be a hole ripped in fabric, but when he turned into a hard piece of ceramic again, it would be a very noticeable chip.

"You shall be called *Chip,*" the angel pronounced. "Let this be a reminder to each of you that the Sons of Adam and Daughters of Eve are broken and in need of their Creator and Savior to be whole again."

The wise men looked at one another. New understanding was dawning in their eyes. They had a purpose indeed—one perhaps greater than they understood.

The angel continued. "The Lord formed the first man from the dust and clay of the earth and breathed life into him. He was perfect until the day the Fallen One came and tempted him and his helpmate. Then they fell into brokenness—that which is called sin. Likewise, you have been formed from clay made by human hands, and the Lord has chosen to use you for his greater purposes. The ways of the Lord are many and mysterious, and he shall use whatever means he chooses to seek and save the lost. So says the Lord."

The angel's eyes narrowed, and his voice became solemn and serious. "Beware of the Fallen One. He and his kind are as powerful and knowledgeable as we angels who are loyal to the Lord, our King. The enemy does not know of your existence. Should they discover you, they will seek your destruction. Do not engage them without the power of the Lord."

"We are small," Harold said. "Why should they care to destroy us? What can we do, anyway?"

The angel frowned. "Yes, you are small, but you are of the Lord. Do not underestimate the power of the Lord to work through you."

Harold nodded and bowed his head in humility. The angel's voice lifted as he proclaimed, "On the twelfth day of each December, your senses, reasoning, and thinking shall return to you. Listen and observe during this time. When the clock reaches midnight as the calendar turns from December 23rd to December 24th each year, you shall change into the form you possess here tonight, and you shall be able to move about freely. It is up to you to discover that which the Lord has for you to do. When daylight comes on the morning of the 24th, your time is up. You shall not come fully to life again until the same time the next year."

The three wise men considered everything the angel had told them. It was a great deal to take in! Yet, their faces already looked happier, even Harold's. They were so glad to know that there was a plan and purpose for their existence.

"The Lord sent me to you tonight so that come your first Christmas, you will be prepared and ready to fulfill your purpose. It is not yet the 24th, so you will return to your original forms for now," said the angel.

"Wait!" said Chip.

"What is it?" asked the angel.

"What's my camel's name?" Chip asked.

The angel's brow rose and a stumped expression came over his face. It was the first time he had shown any real expression—besides sternness—since he had appeared.

Now, angels are not used to being stumped about anything. Humans have created all sorts of images pertaining to angels, and none of them are very close to the real thing. The cute little pictures of angels on everything from calendars to toilet paper hardly show the awesome truth: Angels are the soldiers of God! Real angels act as servants and messengers of the living, all-knowing God. They are powerful warriors who have lived for thousands of years and have fought the Lord's battles while solemnly watching over the human race. There is nothing new to them under the sun.

Yet here, on this dark night in a little store in London, a small Christmas decoration caught an angel off guard with a simple question.

The angel was not sure he had ever used the following words before, but he answered, truthfully and humbly, "I do not know."

The angel looked up as if listening to an unheard voice, then back down to Chip. "The Lord says he will leave it up to you to name your camel."

"Oh, boy! I've got a camel *and* I get to name him!" Chip exclaimed.

The camel seemed pleased too. He nudged Chip on the shoulder playfully.

The angel, who had been so majestic, focused, and serious when he first appeared, actually smiled.

"God bless you, little ones," he said, and then he vanished as quickly as he had appeared. The three wise men and the camel instinctively moved their arms, legs, and bodies back to their original positions as a hard glaze washed over them. They were once more ceramic figurines.

It was not long after the angel left that a police squad car drove down the back alley and noticed that Mr. Clemons's back door was open. Poor Mr. Clemons had to come down to the store in the middle of the night to talk to the police and get the back door fixed, but he was amazed that nothing seemed to be missing. Several of his small antique items had been placed in a bag, but the bag had been left on the floor next to the wise men from the front window. The police said it looked as though the burglars had been scared off by something.

A few days later, Mr. Clemons was walking down a busy London sidewalk carrying a cardboard box. He turned down a narrow street and then up the steps to a large building with the words *Saint Nicholas Orphanage* carved in stone above large wooden double doors.

He pushed the door buzzer and waited…and waited…and waited. Finally, he decided to knock. Within a few seconds, a short, stout man with a white collar opened the door and poked his head out.

"Why, I thought I heard the door a-knockin'!" he said with a thick Scottish brogue and a jovial smile. "Why didn't ye just ring the door buzzer?"

"Ah, well I did push the buzzer—I was wondering if Father Andrew is in. Maybe I should have called first?" said Mr. Clemons.

"Oh, forgive my manners. Please come in, come in." The man opened the door and motioned Mr. Clemons in.

Inside the front door was a large, multipurpose room with a long hallway directly to the left and a matching hallway directly to the right. On the far side of the room was an old pump organ that caught Mr. Clemons's eye. Judging by the placement of the foot pedals, the carved wooden top, and the mirror, his trained eye perceived it to be an early 1800s instrument made in Liverpool. Mixed furniture sat in front of the organ, with none of the individual pieces seeming to match any of the others. The ceilings were high and vaulted, and the walls were covered with crosses, paintings of the Last Supper, and of Jesus surrounded by children, pictures of saints, and other religious artifacts. A few feet inside the door there was a long rectangular oak table placed horizontally across the room. It had a guest signature book on one side and a poinsettia on the other. The table added a kind of break to the room, which helped define the area near the door as an informal entryway.

To the right of the organ, a Nativity scene was arranged on top of another long oak table.

The priest kept talking as he ushered Mr. Clemons inside. "I'm Father Thomas, but the kids call me Scottie, so if ye go askin' for me and ask for Father Thomas, ye may just get one of those funny tilt-o'-the-head, don't-know-what-ye're-talkin'-aboot kinda looks—so it might be best if ye just call me Scottie as well."

"Nice to meet you, Father—um, I mean, Scottie. I am Horace, Horace Clemons." Mr. Clemons extended a handshake.

Father Andrew's voice echoed from the long hallway to the left. "Well, Clem, my good friend, what brings you here?"

"I've got a little present for the orphanage." Clem smiled and held up the box. As Father Andrew approached, Clem set the box on the entry table and pulled out one of the wise men. "I decided to let you have these since you said that your wise men went missing."

"Well, say, isn't that a fine gift!" Scottie said as he reached into the box to pull out another of the wise men. "Oh, fine indeed, fine indeed! These're much nicer than anythin' we're used to. The children will be happy to see we've got some wise men with our Nativity."

"This is very generous of you, Clem. Thank you for thinking of us." Father Andrew shook Mr. Clemons's hand and then nodded over his shoulder. "Come back to the kitchen with me; I'll put some tea on. The cook just made fresh crumpets—we had better test them and make sure they're good enough for the children, don't you think?"

"That sounds fine on a cold day like today," Clem said with a chuckle.

"You two go ahead," said Scottie as he placed the wise men back in the box. "I'll set these little fellas up with the rest of the Nativity scene."

Father Andrew paused and turned back to Scottie. "I forgot to tell you, I don't think our door buzzer is working properly. Would you mind taking a look at it?"

"Sure, sure! Ye go have your tea and crumpets; I'll take care of every-thin'!" Scottie said as he waved them on.

As the other men disappeared, Scottie carried the box across the room. He took the figurines out of the box and set them next to the rest of the Nativity—but there was a problem. The three wise men were a bit out of place. They were much fancier than the rustic, carved wood pieces, and even though they were six inches tall, they were small in comparison to the rest of the figurines. Even the baby Jesus in the manger was almost as big as they were.

"Hmm." Scottie rubbed his chin and studied the situation. "I didn't know ye were *that* much smaller."

As he tried to fit them into the arrangement in a way that wouldn't accentuate their size, he started humming "We Three Kings."

"Hum, hum, hum, hum-hum—hum—hum—hum…"

Scottie let out a burst of laughter. "WEE Three Kings indeed!" he chortled. "*Wee* Three Kings is just what ye are: wee little men that come from afar."

He turned Uncle upside down and looked at the inscription.

"Ha! That is good! Made in China! You *are* from the Orient!" Still chuckling, Scottie picked up his tune. "*Wee* three kings of Orient are… sort of short in our demeanor…hum, hum, hum-hum, hum…we traverse afar."

All of a sudden, Scottie was struck with a great idea. "'Traverse afar'; that's it! They are not small! They are just *far off* and so they *look* small."

With a twinkle in his eye, he nodded to the wise men and said, "I'll be right back."

Minutes later, Scottie came back with a white cloth. He turned the cardboard box upside down and covered it with the cloth. He set the box to the back and off to the side from the rest of the arrangement, creating the illusion that the three wise men were on a far off hill.

"Perfect," Scottie said, stepping back and looking at the whole arrangement. He patted his shirt pocket. "Now for a little break of me own," he said, pulling out a candy bar and unwrapping it.

"Wee three kings of Orient are…not much bigger than a ca-a-ndy bar! Oh, that's a good one! Candy bar! Ha, ha, ha!" His voice echoed down the hall.

Chapter Seven

THE CHRISTMAS CHILD

ncle, Chip, and Harold liked their new home. There was lots of activity in the orphanage, even more so than in the busy London shop. Mr. Clemons had decided to donate them after he received word that the rest of the Nativity would not be coming because of a supply issue at the factory. After the break-in, Mr. Clemons noticed that one of the wise men had a piece broken off at the base, so he would have had to sell them on discount anyway. He thought it better that the children at the orphanage would get some enjoyment out of them.

Uncle, Chip, and Harold had been in the orphanage for only three days, but they had much to talk about. They were still excited about their visit from the angel, and they talked about the special mission that might be in store for them on Christmas Eve.

The organ room, or the activity room as it was called, was an exciting place. In it, the orphanage held Bible studies, children sang around the organ, volunteers read stories, people visited, and kids played board games. It seemed there was always some activity going on. The wise men quickly learned that the south hall was the way to the boys' dorm and the north hall led to the girls' dorm. The kitchen was somewhere behind them on the other side of the wall. When the activity room was quiet, they could hear the muffled sounds of pots and pans banging and the cook singing.

They soon learned many of the children's names, as well as most of the staff and volunteers that worked there. Of all the volunteers, they immediately grew fond of a young lady named Elizabeth, who came in almost every day when she was done with her college classes. She made sure to spend individual time with different children, as well as entertaining the whole group with stories. Some of the stories she made up, some she read from books, and some were true stories of places she had been. The children especially loved hearing about the other children Elizabeth had met on a trip to Uganda. They liked to compare the orphanage in Africa to their own. Elizabeth explained that people and children are the same wherever you go—though their circumstances are often very different.

The wise men listened and paid attention to everything they could see and hear, just as the angel had told them to do. They had no need or desire to sleep, so they spent the nights discussing the events of the day and guessing what the Lord would have them do when they came to life again. It wasn't long before they found out.

The days passed quickly, and soon it was December 23rd. At midnight, they would come to life again. Their anticipation grew minute by minute. They could hear the passing of each hour by the sound of a grandfather clock somewhere down the hall. By nine o'clock, the children were all in bed and the place was quiet. Ten o'clock rolled around slowly, and it was still pretty quiet. Sometime after ten, Father Andrew and Scottie walked through the entry area, talking.

"Well, Andrew, it's about time I get these old bones of mine to bed. I'm not a young lad anymore, ye know."

"The way you crawl around on the floor and laugh and play with the kids is what makes your bones tired, not your age. Don't forget, you're a little younger than I am." The men laughed together, and Father Andrew said, "You go on to bed, Scottie. I feel the need to go and spend some time with God in the sanctuary. I'll see you in the morning."

Out on the streets, it was a cold December night. A petite figure in a worn coat, faded clothes, and a flannel scarf that covered her face moved quickly beneath the streetlights. The figure, who was carrying a large basket wrapped in blankets, stopped across the street from the orphanage.

After looking both ways, she darted across the street. A young woman's frightened eyes peeked over the top of the scarf as she looked back and forth. She set the large basket next to the door, pushed the buzzer three times, ran to the corner of the building, and peered back. Just then, a police car turned and came up the street. The young woman peeked around the corner one more time, looking back toward the door. Her heart pounded nearly out of control at the sight of the police car. With one last glance over her shoulder, she took off quickly down a side street.

The police car passed the orphanage; the officer driving it did not notice the basket on the doorstep.

It was 11:50 p.m. when Uncle heard the baby crying.

"Did you hear that?" he asked the others. Chip and Harold listened. They too could hear the faint sound of a baby whimpering and crying.

"It sounds like it's outside," Harold decided after listening intently for another minute.

"Who would have a baby out this late?" wondered Chip.

"Who indeed," said Uncle. He braced himself in the face of his growing excitement. *This could be it—our purpose—the mission we've been looking for. There is a baby out there who needs our help!*

Dong, dong, dong… the clock started counting down to midnight.

With every sound of the clock, the three wise men could feel a warm sensation wash over their bodies. They started to move and wiggle as they became unfrozen from their hardened forms. Just like at Clemons's Store, the camel was the first to be up and moving. And just like before, he jumped right off the edge of the table.

"Camel! Wait for me! Come back here!" Chip commanded. The only response was a grunt from below.

"You know, if you would give him a name, maybe he would listen a little better—he obviously doesn't want to come to 'Hey you; hey camel!'" said Harold.

Chip had been trying to think of a name, but it was so hard to find the one that was *just right.* The camel obviously agreed. Several of Chip's suggestions had already been grunted down in disapproval.

Moments later, Chip, Harold, and Uncle were completely transformed. They moved to the end of the table where they were able to swing down, grab the spiraled table leg, and corkscrew down to the floor.

"This way!" Uncle said.

They darted across the floor and stopped underneath the long table that divided the entry from the rest of the room. They listened. The crying was a little louder here, but still muffled.

The camel wandered out from behind a potted plant, sniffing the air like a hound dog on the chase. He cocked his head, listened, and then headed straight to the large wooden front doors. The camel lifted both of his front hooves onto the door and looked back at the three wise men.

"Good boy, camel!" Chip said with pride. "I think he's telling us that the crying is coming from the other side of that door."

They joined the camel at the door. Uncle dropped to his stomach and peeked through a small crack.

"I can see something! It looks like the bottom of a wicker basket—like the one that robber trapped us with!"

"Burglar," Harold corrected.

Chip shot a disapproving glance at Harold.

"Sorry," Harold said.

"Someone left a baby in a basket on the doorstep! We've got to help it," Uncle said.

One by one, they raised their heads and looked up at the locked doorknob.

"Climb on," said Chip as he crawled up onto his camel's back.

Chip stood on the camel, Harold climbed up and stood on Chip's shoulders, and Uncle climbed all three to stand on Harold's shoulders.

"Ugh! I can't reach! It's up too high." Uncle stretched a little more, but in his fervent desire to reach the lock above the doorknob, he leaned too far to the side. "Oh no!" Harold cried as Uncle's weight pulled him over. They all tumbled to the ground.

They looked around the room. The heavy oak chairs would be too big for them to move.

Outside, the baby was crying harder.

"We need to get help!" said Chip. He jumped on his camel again, this time in a riding position. "Go find the priest, camel!"

And off the camel ran with Chip hanging on for dear life and Harold and Uncle running after them.

"He really must think of a name for the poor beast," Harold puffed as they tried to keep up.

They ran down the hall and then turned left into another hall. A sign on the wall pointed the way to the sanctuary. The camel screeched to a halt in front of a pair of heavy wooden double doors adorned with small panes of stained glass. Camel motioned with his head for Chip to look up. A decorative, carved wooden sign above the doors read, *The Father Timothy Memorial Chapel.* Chip read the sign and looked back at his camel.

"You can read?"

The camel nodded as if to say, *Of course I can.*

Chip hopped off and began pushing on the door with all his might. Harold and Uncle caught up and added their own weight to the effort. They pushed and strained and pushed some more. The door didn't budge.

"Push harder," Chip encouraged. They pushed again. Still nothing.

The camel let out a loud grunt, and the three wise men stopped pushing and turned their attention to him. He was pointing with his nose toward the door handle. Right above it was a small brass plaque that read *Pull.*

"Oh, great. We'll never get this door open," said Chip, feeling defeated. Even he couldn't think of a positive thing to say now.

Down the hall, Uncle spied another option.

"Come on!" he yelled, running down to a large metal grate covering an air vent on the wall. He grabbed the side and pulled. One of the screws was stripped, and it pulled out easily.

The grate pulled away from the wall, making a gap wide enough for the wise men to pass through.

As Harold slipped inside, he eyed the anatomy of the building. "Good observation, Uncle! I suspect that these airways were built into the walls to allow air to circulate before the days of modern air-conditioning. I'll bet we will find that the sanctuary has no windows that open."

Chip shook his head and mumbled to himself, "How does he come up with stuff like that?" He looked back at his camel, who was stuck—his belly was too wide to fit through easily. Chip looked at the other two as they moved down the corridor, then back to his camel. He was torn between whether to follow or help tug his camel through the crack. Quickly making a decision, Chip held the palm of his hand up to the camel's face. "Stay! I'll come back for you."

The camel rolled his eyes and snorted his annoyance at being treated like a dumb animal.

Their feet pitter-pattered on the one-hundred-and fifty-year-old stone as they ran through the dusty passage. Cobwebs reached out and clung to them. Light fell across the passage from another grate, and they ran to it and looked out. It gave them a view into the sanctuary; they could see rows of beautifully carved oak pews as old and sturdy as the stone under their feet, but no sign of the priest. Uncle was the first one there, and he pushed against the grate, but the screws were tight. He saw another light up ahead and ran to it. This grate was tight too. The others caught up to him, and they all pushed together, but the grate wouldn't budge.

Chip was gasping for breath. "We're at a dead end," he said. It was true. The passageway was blocked by tin ductwork that must have been installed during modern remodeling. It curved, branched, and went straight up into another passageway that disappeared into the ceiling.

The three wise men peered through the grate into the sanctuary. Father Andrew was on his knees, praying in front of the altar. "And please, Lord, bless the children, and find each of them a loving family where they can go. Lord, speak to my heart your will…"

"Andrew!"

A voice echoed through the sanctuary and caught Father Andrew by surprise. He lifted his head, his eyebrows arching. "Who's there?" he asked, looking up and around him. He saw no one.

"Lord, Father, is it you?" he said hesitantly.

The voice echoed again. "No, it's Uncle, I'm…"

Harold quickly put his hand over Uncle's mouth.

"Lord…*Uncle?*" Father Andrew said, confused.

Then a deep, serious voice echoed loudly through the sanctuary.

"Listen carefully: this is a servant of the Lord speaking. You must go now to the front door. There you will find a child lying in a basket."

Father Andrew was growing suspicious. "Who's there? What kind of game are you playing?"

Just then, the camel, who had finally managed to push through the grate, came running at top speed down the corridor. In fact, he was running so fast that when he tried to stop he slid headfirst right into the tin ductwork. The ductwork shook and reverberated all the way up the wall, making a horrible sound that echoed in the sanctuary like thunder. Father Andrew's eyes grew big.

After seeing the look on Father Andrew's face, and taking advantage of the camel's clumsy mishap, Harold boomed, "GO NOW!"

Father Andrew stumbled on his robe as he jumped to his feet. He raced out of the sanctuary and down the hall to the entry. His hands shaking, he fumbled with the lock and opened the door.

There, on the steps in front of him, was a basket covered with a bundle of baby blankets. He pulled the blanket back, and a pair of bright blue baby eyes looked back up at him.

"Well, I'll be!" Father Andrew was astonished. "Let's get you in, out of the cold."

Once inside, Father Andrew cradled the baby close to his chest. Other than being a little bit cold, the baby seemed fine and healthy. He blinked repeatedly in the bright light and moved his head from side to side, taking in his surroundings. At Father Andrew's warm touch and soothing voice, the little one sniffled, took a deep breath, and relaxed into the secure arms that held him.

Scottie came down a set of stairs just off the hallway, rubbing his eyes.

"What 'tis going on down here? A terrible rumblin' noise shook me right out of a deep sleep!"

"You heard it too?" Father Andrew replied.

"What was it?" asked Scottie. His eyes grew big as he looked at Father Andrew's bundle.

Father Andrew smiled, holding out the baby for him to see. "A miracle, that's what it was. It was a miracle!"

Chapter Eight

WAX FOOTPRINTS

That first Christmas Eve, the three wise men watched from the shadows as Father Andrew told and retold the story of the mysterious voice and the thunder that had alerted him to the baby on the doorstep. Scottie heard the story first, then the police officer who came to investigate, then the orphanage nurse who came to check the baby's health, and then the social worker who was called by the police officer.

Together, Scottie and the police officer discovered that the door buzzer was not working. Scottie had fixed it a few days before, but one of the wires had shorted out again. The baby would have frozen if it hadn't been for "the servant of the Lord" (or "the angel," as it was retold) who alerted Father Andrew.

The night was wonderfully mysterious and heartwarming, and everyone who heard the story of the miracle Christmas baby got caught up in it. The story spread from person to person and made the newspapers as well. Yet, the little baby boy was a mystery. The only clue to his identity was a note pinned to one of the blankets:

PLEASE TAKE CARE OF JW. I LOVE HIM VERY MUCH.

That night, the three wise men decided it was best to let God have the credit for anything they might do in the future. They would take care to remain unseen as they fulfilled their future missions. After all, they reasoned, it was God who had given them life in the first place, so the credit did truly belong to him.

It was exciting and rewarding for them to see how the people wanted—*needed*—a miracle to believe in. In the wee hours of the morning, the three wise men and the camel managed to find their places back atop the table next to the Nativity. They enjoyed the feeling of a job well done while they waited for daylight to come and turn them into ceramic once more.

Right before the sunlight peeked through the window, Chip perked up. "I've got it!" He looked proudly at his camel. "I shall call you Thunder!"

The camel grunted, as camels do, and nodded his approval. And that is how Thunder got his name.

Over the next five years, the wise men and Thunder continued to complete Christmas Eve missions. One year, someone forgot to blow out a candle that had been left on a windowsill. The candle was in a glass jar, but the wax had burned all the way down to the bottom, and the wick was a little too long. The base of the glass grew so hot that the painted wooden windowsill began to smolder. It surely would have developed into a dangerous fire if not for the miniature crusaders and their trusty camel roaming the halls that night.

Actually, Thunder did most of the work. As Chip, Harold, and Uncle developed an elaborate plan to bring a ladle full of water from the kitchen, hoist it up on a string to the windowsill, and use it to put out the fire, Thunder was busy working in the background. Somehow, he managed to get himself from the floor up to the windowsill—they're still not sure exactly how he did it.

Uncle was the first one to notice.

"What's your camel doing?" he asked, pointing up to the windowsill.

The other two looked just in time to see the glass jar burst and a small plume of fire beginning to form on the surface of the wood. Thunder was already on the windowsill. His jaw and lips started moving as if he had peanut butter stuck to the roof of his mouth, and then, *P-tooie,* he spit an impressive wad of saliva.

The fire hissed, died down, and flared up again. Two, three more times, Thunder spit. *P-tooie, p-tooie, p-tooie!* Then he rushed in and stomped the rest of the fire out with his hooves. The wise men all looked at each other in amazement.

"Well, I guess where there's thunder, there's rain," Chip said proudly.

The next morning, it wasn't hard for the people to figure out what happened to the candle. They were glad it had "burned itself out." The only thing that puzzled them was the set of small wax hoof prints running across the windowsill.

None of their missions was as dramatic as the miracle of the Christmas child, but that would change. In fact, all of their further adventures went unnoticed by anyone but the wise men themselves—until their fifth Christmas.

Chapter Nine

CHRISTMAS WISH

Five years had passed, and JW had not been adopted. The wise men watched with amazement each year as he grew and changed. They were, in fact, growing wiser with each year's twelve days of learning. Positioned as they were in the orphanage's activity room, they had plenty of opportunities to hear Bible lessons, Christmas songs, and hymns. They also learned about human nature, and they discovered how children and adults can grow and change.

Their favorite volunteer, Elizabeth, grew from a starry-eyed, impressionable teen who had just begun college into a responsible young woman. Busy with life and work, she didn't volunteer as much as she used to, but her heart always brought her back to the orphanage around Christmastime. She had grown fond of many of the children, and she was always happy to hear when one of them found a home. She had grown fond of JW too, and she just couldn't understand why no family had stepped forward to adopt such an adorable little boy. His sandy blond hair, blue eyes, and inquisitive nature were only some of the characteristics that made him a joy to be around. He asked sincere and challenging questions for one so young, wanting to know how things worked and why things happened. Things that other children took for granted, or never thought to ask, occupied JW's mind.

"How come God won't let us see him, so I can give him a hug?"

"Who was Adam and Eve's doctor?"

"Where did they keep the termites on Noah's ark?"

Five years earlier, Elizabeth had been sure that he would be adopted right away, especially with all of the attention brought about by his miraculous rescue from the cold of the night. She often hoped in her heart that he would be gone—off with a new family—when she stopped in sporadically throughout the year. But he was always still there.

At the start of the wise men's fifth Christmas, someone had decided to be a little more creative with the decorations. When they awoke and became aware on December 12th of that year, they found that they were on display in the sanctuary instead of the front activity room. They sat at table height at the front of the room, next to the chapel. Staying true to Scottie's original design, they were afar from the rest of the Nativity scene on a long display table.

Chip was the first to speak.

"Where do you suppose we are? This room doesn't look familiar."

"Chip, if you will note the architecture, we are clearly in one of the oldest rooms in the orphanage. I theorize that this was the original chapel, and the rest of the building structure was added at later dates and phases as the purpose of the building grew and changed."

Before Harold could dive into his more complex theories about architectural design, Chip cut him off in mid-thought.

"Thanks, Harold! You're right, we are in the small chapel—I remember it now. I have just never seen the room from this angle."

The chapel's hand-carved oak pews showed their age only because of the different shades of color where years of rumps and shoulders had caused them to lose some of their varnish. Waves of dark stain with repeating light patches rippled up and down the long pews on each side of the room.

The center aisle started at the heavy wooden double doors at the back of the room and led straight up to the platform where an ornate altar was the center of attention. An equally ornate podium stood to one side of the room. Like the pews, the podium had been carved by hands long passed from this earth. Stretching to the left of the podium was a half wall where people received communion, topped by lacquered wood used as a resting place for hands clasped in prayer.

Directly behind the six-foot table where the Nativity decorations were placed, another half wall shielded an organ with brass pipes that reached an impressive eight feet into the air. The woodwork surrounding the pipes and the body of the organ was the most ornately carved piece of antiquity in the whole room. Behind the organ, an inconspicuous doorway led to a back hall where the organist could come and go without disrupting the chapel services.

On December 14th, Father Andrew was in the sanctuary straightening hymnals and dusting pews with a damp rag when Elizabeth entered from the back of the room.

"Father Andrew, do you have a minute?"

He turned, startled. "Oh, Elizabeth, it's you. I haven't seen you in here since…since…well it's been a while. What can I do for you, child?"

Guilt was written on her face. "I'm sorry. I've just been so busy."

"Oh nonsense, don't be sorry. I wasn't trying to make you feel guilty; I was just trying to say how glad I am to see you. Come in and sit down," Father Andrew said. He gestured to a pew with his still-damp dusting rag.

"Thank you, Father. I wanted to talk to you about something—something important."

"Go ahead," said Father Andrew, sitting down and giving her his full attention.

"Well, do you remember the boy—I mean, the young man—I met five and a half years ago when I was in Uganda?"

"Yes, yes, the American boy."

"Right, well, Hiram and I became pen pals and have stayed in touch all of this time. We have occasionally talked on the phone—but we really became best friends through our letters."

Father Andrew stayed quiet and attentive while she paused.

"Well, anyway, to make a long story short, he surprised me with a visit a month ago." Elizabeth smiled and blushed slightly, looking down at her hands in her lap.

"He flew all the way from America to see you?" Father Andrew asked.

"Yes, well…" She smiled again. "We had a great time together for the week that he was here. He met my parents, we toured the city and saw all the sights, had dinners together, we held hands…and…" Elizabeth's voice softened, and her gaze fixed as her attention drifted back into that week. "…we kissed." She immediately snapped back to attention, embarrassed that the last part had slipped out. "Oh, I'm sorry Father, I…"

Father Andrew patted her shoulder, ignoring the dusty smudge his rag left. "Elizabeth, Elizabeth, shh! I am a priest. I have heard a lot worse things than…" He smiled. "…than two young people falling in love."

She smiled. Even though he *was* a priest, she could see that he understood what she was trying to say—what was in her heart.

"Yes, Father, you're right. I do love him."

"And does he love you?"

Her eyes lit in response. "Yes. That's actually what I came to talk to you about. He called me last night. He said he is flying back to London this week to ask me to marry him. He said, 'Don't answer me now—whether the answer is yes or no, I want you to say it to me in person. If you say no, it's okay; I'll turn and walk away knowing I gave you plenty of time to think it over.' He's so wonderful; I've never met anyone like him."

"And what was it you wanted to talk to *me* about?" Father Andrew said, smiling, both eyebrows raised.

Elizabeth exhaled and rolled her head to relieve the tension in her neck. She looked up as though searching for the words—and then out poured a ramble of thoughts.

"Oh, Father Andrew, I want to say yes, but it's so sudden! I just started a new job…and what if he wants me to move to America? How could I leave my home, my family, the orphanage, the children, my friends…everything! I…I am just so excited and so scared all at the same time. What should I do, Father? I am just so confused."

Father Andrew sat up a little straighter and let his smile fade into a more solemn look.

"I cannot tell you to marry him or not to marry him. You will have to make that decision on your own. I *can* tell you that any successful marriage is built first on love and then on sacrifice. Both of you will have to sacrifice something in order to have a successful marriage. Not just in the beginning, but year after year, at one time or another. Love always involves sacrifice."

Elizabeth had tears in her eyes, and she breathed a heavy sigh.

"I just wish I could know for sure how everything will work out."

Father Andrew laid aside his dust rag and reached an open hand to Elizabeth. "Let's pray about this. God knows how everything will work out. You will just have to trust in him to lead you."

As Elizabeth took Father Andrew's hand and they prayed, Chip made a sniffling sound and said, "She's going to get married. Little Elizabeth is going to get married." *Sniff, sniff.*

"Are you crying, Chip?" Harold inquired.

Sniff. Chip replied quickly, "No, I'm not crying. I'm ceramic—ceramic doesn't cry."

"Well, she hasn't decided to marry him yet—she hasn't made up her mind," Harold observed, logical as always.

"Oh yes, she has," answered Uncle confidently. "Her heart is *definitely* going to get married, even if her head hasn't figured it out yet."

"And you're an expert on love, hmm?" said Harold dryly.

Elizabeth and Father Andrew finished their prayer with an "amen."

Father Andrew sat a little straighter, smiled, and said, "Hey, I hear you are coming in very early the morning of Christmas Eve to help with the big breakfast feed. Are you sure you'll be able to get up that early?"

Elizabeth laughed and pulled a tissue from her pocket to dry her eyes. "Yes, I am. I may not like getting up that early, but you can count on me!"

December 23rd was a long day. They could hear activities taking place in different parts of the building, but there wasn't much happening in the sanctuary. The wise men noticed the passing of time much more than they wished to. All the evening was quiet in the dimly lit sanctuary. Then, at around 11:45 p.m., the door at the back of the sanctuary creaked open. A little boy in pajamas walked up the center aisle carrying a tattered blue blanket.

"Hey, look! It's JW," Chip announced.

All three wise men watched and listened as JW walked right up and stood in front of them. His hair was sticking up on one side of his head, and they could tell by his eyes that he had been sleeping. He looked over all the figurines in the Nativity, and then his eyes fell back to the figure of baby Jesus in the manger. JW clasped his hands together, closed his eyes tight, and prayed aloud.

"Thank you for saving me when I was a baby, and thank you for Father Andrew and for Scottie, and for all the people who take care of us. This is a nice place, but Jesus, all I really want for Christmas is a family. What I really want is a mom and dad and maybe a brother. I'd be a good boy and not cause any problems if someone would just give me a chance. Well, thank you, God. That's all I wanted to say. Amen."

JW turned around and dragged his blanket to the front pew where he sat and stared back at the Nativity scene with tired little eyes.

"This must be our mission. We have to find him a family," Uncle declared triumphantly.

"How are we going to do that? Maybe God wants us to tell him not to get his hopes up, that these things take time," Harold said.

"We shouldn't talk directly to him. Remember, we decided a long time ago that talking to people wasn't a good idea—but I agree with Uncle," Chip pitched in. "We should at least try to find him a family."

Harold was still cautious. "It's the middle of the night and we only have a short time; how do we know anything about families? What if he ended up with someone who wasn't very nice?"

"Remember the message preached last Sunday? The work is ours to do—the results belong to God," Uncle replied.

"We at least have to *try* to find him a family," said Chip, turning his head toward Harold.

Harold raised his hands. "Okay, okay, let's see what we can do."

"But no talking to the kid, right?" added Chip.

Uncle cleared his throat and talked silently through clenched teeth. "Uh, guys—we—are—*moving.*"

They all froze and turned their eyeballs toward JW, who was still sitting there looking straight ahead—straight at them, in fact.

JW hopped off the pew and walked up to the three wise men.

"Hi, I'm JW. Are you really going to find me a family? What're your names?"

All of one mind, they held their breath and tried not to move. But when you go for three hundred and sixty-four days a year without being able to move, it's very hard to stand still when you *are* able to move.

Just then, Chip realized that he couldn't feel Thunder kneeling behind him.

JW's hand moved up and past the heads of the wise men. "You're a nice little camel; what's your name?" he asked. The three wise men moved their heads slowly. There was Thunder, rubbing and caressing his way around JW's hand like a lonely house cat.

All three exhaled at the same time.

"Great, now what!" exclaimed Chip.

JW smiled. "Are you guys playing a game? Is it like freeze tag? I love freeze tag."

"No, we're not playing a game," said Uncle, looking sternly up at JW. "How much of what we said did you hear, anyway?"

JW pointed at Chip. "He said you're not supposed to talk to people, and then that one said it's the middle of the night…"

Uncle interrupted. "Okay, okay, JW, so you pretty much heard everything."

"Are you really going to find me a family?" JW asked again.

"Yes," Uncle said. He cleared his throat and said in a reassuring voice, "Well, I mean, we are going to try."

"Are you elves?" JW asked.

"Forgive us for being so rude," interjected Harold in his most dignified tone. "We should have introduced ourselves. No, we are not elves.

We are wise men. I am Harold, this is Uncle, and over here is Chip. Oh, and our camel is named Thunder."

JW looked at the rest of the Nativity, his blue eyes wide but not doubtful. "Do they talk too?"

"Um, no, just us three and the camel—well, I mean the camel, Thunder, he doesn't talk…he, uh, mostly spits and grunts. But he's one of us," explained Uncle.

All three talked to JW a while longer, briefly explaining who and *what* they were as best as they could. They assured him that they would do all they could to find him a family. Then they sent a hopeful JW back to bed and went to work brainstorming what the plan should be.

"I remember seeing a file cabinet in the adoption director's office that had applications of prospective parents," Uncle noted.

Harold nodded. "That will be a good place to start. Let's get into the office and look through the files. We may be able to find a family that way."

"Come on, let's get moving." Chip motioned to the doorway behind the organ.

After a short excursion up some stairs, under the door of the locked office, and into a file cabinet, the wise men and Thunder set up their operation on top of the adoption director's desk. The air in the room was stale with a hint of old-building musk.

The *tick, tick, tick* of the clock on the wall kept pace with their concentrated efforts. The only time they paused was to listen to the various creaks, groans, and whistles of air that were familiar noises in the old building—familiar, but still a possible warning of someone moving about in the hall. Each time they heard something they would pause, look up, and listen. They would set back to work when they were satisfied it was just the melody of the building.

The files included a lot of information about prospective parents and their families. Together, the wise men read through thirty-three adoption applicant files and narrowed their choices down to the most worthy candidates. It was 3 a.m. when they finished.

"Now what?" asked Harold.

Uncle thought for a moment. "Why don't we leave the files on the director's desk with a note that says these are the best candidates for him to contact on behalf of JW?"

Harold grunted. "He's the adoption director. He should already know that."

"I've got a better idea," said Chip. "Let's call the families ourselves. We've already broken our 'don't talk to people' rule, and they won't know it's us."

"It's the middle of the night," Harold reminded him.

"And we've never used a phone," Uncle added.

"How hard can it be?" Chip walked across the desk and pushed the phone off the receiver. It wasn't much smaller than he was. "What's the first number?"

"Are you really going to do this?" Uncle asked.

Chip just looked at him impatiently.

"Okay, fine, the first number is…"

Harold and Uncle took turns reading the names and numbers to Chip. Thunder used his hooves to push the buttons on the phone, and Chip did the talking.

It didn't go very well. Even the people who were polite were very confused, having been awakened so early in the morning. After several failed attempts, Harold said, "Let me do the talking."

"Hu-hmm. This worked once before," said Harold, clearing his baritone voice.

A man's groggy voice answered the phone finally. "Hello?"

"Listen carefully," Harold intoned in his deep, solemn voice. "This is a servant of the Lord, and I have a message for you. There is a child named JW who needs a family—"

The gravelly voice on the other end of the phone didn't let Harold get any further. He lectured him on the rudeness of making prank calls in the middle of the night, told Harold that he should be ashamed of himself, and angrily slammed the phone down.

Harold turned to look at the other two wise men.

"Mark him off the list—he's much too angry!"

None of the other calls went much better. At last, they tidied up the office the best they could and headed back to the sanctuary with their heads bent in defeat.

In the dim light of the sanctuary, they were surprised to see JW curled up with his blanket, sleeping in the front pew. The small boy stirred when they came back.

"Did you find me a family for Christmas?" he asked, swinging his bare feet down so that they hung over the pew.

Thunder's head hung low, and the three wise men's defeated expressions grew even sadder.

Chip spoke first.

"We tried, we really tried, but we don't have very good news. You see, we…we…"

Harold tried to help. "What Chip is trying to say is—we don't know. We talked to some people. But we're not sure that they really understood what we were trying to tell them."

Uncle added, "You have to keep faith. We don't know—maybe one of those people will come down here to find out who was calling them in the wee hours of the morning, and things will work out. God has a way of making things work out." He forced a brave smile.

JW dropped off the pew, shuffled to his feet, and forced a small smile in return.

"I've been told that before. It's okay. Thank you for trying." JW's voice was so sad and disappointed that the wise men found themselves having to swallow big lumps in their throats.

"I really wish we could tell you something for sure. I'm sorry," said Chip.

There was an awkward silence until Harold spoke again.

"JW, our time is almost up. Would you mind lifting us back up on the table where we belong?"

JW smiled, a more authentic smile this time. "Sure." He lifted them one by one onto the table, and as he did, he thanked them again for trying to help.

"You know I just want a real home and a real family. I want a mom who will tuck me in and read me stories—and a dad to wrestle with and maybe take me fishing."

"That sounds nice," Uncle replied.

"I know I am bad sometimes, and sometimes I fight with the other kids, but maybe if I had a dad, he could teach me how to be better." JW's face fell. "Maybe God's not happy with me."

"No, that's not it!" Chip said. He stuck out his foot to show the missing piece in his garment and blinked away the tears in his eyes. "This torn bit is a chip when I am ceramic. It's broken—that's why I'm called Chip. Remember, we are *all* a little broken. God loves those who are broken, and he will never give up on them—he will never give up on you!"

"JW—who are you talking to?" came a friendly female voice from the back of the chapel.

It was Elizabeth. She had come in early, as promised, to help with cooking a large community breakfast. When she arrived, the monitor from the boys' dorm was frantically looking for JW, who was missing from his bed. Elizabeth had joined the search. Before long, she had poked her head into the sanctuary and seen JW at the front of the chapel.

She had been about to rush to him when she thought she heard a man's voice—faint, but definitely a man's voice. She stopped and listened before saying anything. She could hear JW clearly as he talked, and it broke her heart to hear how desperately he wanted a family. And then, there it was again—the faint sound of a man's voice. But she couldn't see anyone else in the sanctuary!

"JW," she asked again, "who are you talking to?"

"Just my friends," JW answered as Elizabeth walked down the aisle and came up behind him.

She looked over his head at the Nativity scene and then glanced around the chapel, wondering where the other voice had come from.

"What friends?" she asked.

JW stepped aside and introduced the three wise men. "This is Uncle—he got his name from the guy who painted him at a factory in China. This is Harold, like in 'Hark the Herald Angels Sing,' and that's Chip, because he has a chip on his robe and the angel told him to remember that people are broken too—just like me—and that is Thunder; he's a camel. They all work for God." JW smiled innocently and looked back up at Elizabeth.

She looked puzzled. "I thought I heard voices—was there someone else in here with you?"

"Just them. They're real—see?" JW reached out and touched Thunder. His coarse hair had turned hard, cold, and smooth. JW then picked up Thunder and Chip, who were now stuck together as one piece of ceramic.

"Oh, well. They *were* real. It must be morning already," JW said, frowning.

Elizabeth reached down, picked up JW, and gave him a hug.

"You have quite the imagination. Come on now. Everyone is worried about you—let's get you back to the boys' dorm." She smiled.

JW laid his head on Elizabeth's shoulder as she carried him out of the chapel.

Though none of them knew it, that night in the chapel was the last time the wee three kings would see the orphanage—and when they saw JW next, it would be years later and halfway around the world.

Chapter Ten

AND THE BLIND WILL SEE

Springtime at the orphanage always included annual spring-cleaning. It was a time when the children, staff, and volunteers cleaned, straightened, and organized the orphanage from top to bottom. This included going through everything in the storage rooms, closets, cupboards, and cabinets. Spring-cleaning at the orphanage always ended with an updated inventory and tabletops full of items to be sold in the annual yard sale. Each year, the children were rewarded for their help with a fun activity the following weekend.

This year during the cleaning process, a volunteer discovered the worn and tattered Nativity scene and the mismatched wise men. She was an aristocratic woman with fine tastes. Her thin-rimmed glasses hung on a chain around her neck when they weren't perched on the tip of her nose.

"Oh, no-o-o. No, no, no, these simply will not work." Her tone was nasally, and the dismissive flick of her wrist looked very 'nasally' as well.

She looked down her long pointed nose, put her glasses on, and raised her eyebrows as she examined the state of the Nativity set.

"What would the society ladies think if I were to give them a tour at Christmastime and they saw *these*?"

Her head moved slowly from side to side.

"Just look at this Nativity! It is positively dastardly!" She paced back and forth a couple of steps with one hand on her hip and the other cocked at the elbow with her hand flung up by her shoulder. Though no one was there to see her talking to herself, it certainly looked as though she was putting on a show.

She paused and scanned the whole assortment again. She cocked her head and squinted intently at the three wise men.

"Well now, these pieces are fetching."

She picked up Harold and ran her fingers over his detailing, then picked up Uncle in the other hand and peered back and forth at them like a mother-in-law trying to decide which dinnerware her son's wife should purchase.

Both pieces must have met her approval, because she looked genuinely impressed. She gingerly set them down and picked up the last piece, Chip and Thunder.

As she looked down her nose, her pleased expression didn't change until her finger rubbed over the broken piece in Chip's robe. Her eyes narrowed.

Aghast, she quickly put the piece back on the table, which rattled from the light thud.

"I must! Yes, I must make a sacrifice here! I will donate a brand-new Nativity set for the orphanage to have next Christmas. No, I will donate two—one that the children can play with and a nice one that no one is allowed to touch."

On the day of the yard sale, crowds of people from the neighborhood milled around tables laden with toys, blankets, clothes, kitchen items, and more. Throughout the year, the orphanage received donations of all kinds—so many, in fact, that they started running out of storage space to keep it all. That was how the annual yard sale had started. People knew that if their donation could not be used by the children or the organization, it would be sold. Either way, the orphanage benefited.

The wise men were set out on a table with lots of other mismatched items. Being that it was springtime, they didn't draw much attention. Most people simply weren't thinking of Christmas. The wise men were continually overlooked—until a handsome young man in a sailor's uniform walked up. He was actually looking for something Christmassy.

Riley Taylor was a crewmember on the HMS *Tireless,* one of Great Britain's nuclear submarines. He had one more week of leave before he headed back to sea. Nuclear submarines can stay submerged for months at a time, so the crewmembers do creative things on board to help pass the time. Each year on the HMS *Tireless,* they threw a Christmas in July celebration complete with dinner, gift exchange, carol singing, and decorating. Riley bought the wise men as soon as he saw them. They would be great for the gift exchange!

Weeks after setting sail, the crew of the HMS *Tireless* were making preparations for their annual Christmas in July celebration in between their regular assigned duties. Their navy duties kept them plenty busy, but fun distractions were good for morale. This year, the celebration was greatly anticipated because they were doing a deep-sea ice exercise— they would actually be passing beneath the North Pole. The ice exercise demonstrated the British submarine fleet's ability to navigate freely in international waters, including under the ice in the Arctic Ocean, arguably one of the harshest maritime environments on Earth.

Living cocooned in a vessel about ten meters wide and as far from end to end as a pro can kick a football was a harsh environment in itself. The submariners spent weeks without glimpsing daylight, breathing fresh air, or speaking to their loved ones.

Young men doing their various duties moved in and out of cramped metal spaces. Sterile white and gray paint covered most of the inner structure, and tubular steel and cables ran along walls and ceilings. Every inch was engineered with calculated precision. Passageways were designed for the practical function of moving from one space to another—not with comfort in mind. Yet, white-uniformed sailors slunk expertly though round metal doorways and narrow hallways, often passing one another, miraculously, without making contact, their faces stoic as they went about their duties. In other parts of the underwater capsule, others relaxed or snoozed in their bunks, waiting for their next six-hour shift to begin.

"This is your captain speaking," came a voice over the submarine's intercom system. "I would like to congratulate all of you for a job well done as we practiced our maneuvers under the Arctic ice shelf this week. Everything went as planned."

Kkkkrt. The intercom system keyed off, then came on again.

"I know there have been rumors that we might conduct a surprise surfacing at the North Pole tomorrow, and I am sorry to tell you that those rumors are false." The captain waited as a disappointed "awww" from the crew echoed through the vessel.

The captain continued, "Those rumors are false because we are actually doing the surfacing today!"

A collective "Yeah!" rang through the ship.

The captain let the cheers die down before he continued. "We have identified two naturally occurring leads in the ice about .8 kilometers from each other at the North Pole. Today we will be surfacing through one of those holes." The crew cheered again as the captain paused for effect. Leads, or gaps in the ice, were their only chance to get above the water.

The captain keyed the intercom system again. "Our Christmas in July celebration is scheduled for two days from now, but I was thinking—what better way to start a Christmas celebration than at the North Pole?"

The captain paused for effect once more. "And what would a celebration be without inviting some friends?"

Crewmembers throughout the vessel shrugged their shoulders and raised their eyebrows at one another, wondering what in the world he meant by *that*. After all, they were literally at the end of the earth, in the middle of nowhere in one of the harshest places in the natural world.

The captain continued. "I mentioned that we have identified two holes. Well, that works out grand, because our friends from America on the USS *Hampton* nuclear submarine will need a place to surface if they are going to join our party!"

Mouths dropped open in stunned disbelief all over the submarine.

"You heard me right," the voice over the intercom continued. "We will be doing joint maneuvers with the Americans. But before we get started with official business, we will be surfacing at the North Pole for a little gift exchange. Merry Christmas, men. Merry Christmas!"

The vessel exploded with whoops and hollers and cheers.

Crewmembers had been crammed on board the submarines for weeks, so they were more than happy to get out and take a stroll in the bright white beauty of the Arctic wilderness. As they ascended into the sunlight, squinting and breathing the cold air, the submariners lifted their hands and shouted greetings to the American crew already waiting on the snow. On the frozen, snow-packed ice they shared steaming cups of hot chocolate and coffee along with a meal. Laughing and joking, they exchanged gifts and stories. It was a day the crews of both ships would never forget. They would tell their children and grandchildren about how they'd had Christmas in July at the North Pole.

That gift exchange is how the wise men came to be in the hands of an American Navy first mate named Gary Martin from his new friend Riley. For the next few months, the wise men stayed safely tucked away inside Gary's locker on board the USS *Hampton*.

On December 12th, just like in all the years before, the three wise men awakened. They were in complete darkness other than a few slivers of light filtering in through the slits in the locker door.

"Why are we all tied up and bound like this?" Chip wondered aloud. "I think I'm taped to this shelf."

"Perhaps someone's afraid we might escape," teased Harold.

Uncle chuckled. "You should see your camel. He has a big piece of foam taped to his head—it makes it look like the two of you have matching turbans."

Thunder only grunted in disgust.

Without warning, the door swung open, giving them a view of a young navy man and his cramped sleeping quarters. They could also see each other more clearly; Gary had them wrapped with padding made from foam and taped to the top shelf. Submarines have very strict rules and procedures for guaranteeing that nothing on board makes a sound.

Great lengths are taken to make sure there is no rubbing, rattling, or noise of any kind. Even the smallest clink of two ceramic figures hitting one another could be enough to alert an enemy submarine of their location underwater.

Being on a submarine with a bunch of young sailors gave the wise men the opportunity to learn many new words—and to learn more about where they were. They were very concerned and confused about how they'd ended up here. Why did they leave the orphanage? Would their lives always be full of such mysteries? Mostly they were sad, knowing that they might never have a chance to hear what had happened to JW. Had he found a family? Had their efforts done any good? Through conversations they overheard, they figured out that they were on a nuclear submarine called the USS *Hampton.* Uncle, Chip, and Harold were all glad to hear the young sailors talking about the upcoming docking for a short Christmas break.

Unlike the British submarine, which was on the start of a long tour of duty at sea, the Americans were coming to the end of many months on duty. They would dock to be resupplied, and some of the crew would go off the sub while new replacements came on.

Somehow, the thought of a clumsy miniature camel running around a military vessel with nuclear missiles on board made the three wise men a little bit nervous. So they were glad to hear that they would be going ashore with Gary before Christmas Eve came.

Gary and his crewmates took leave on December 19th after their submarine docked at Point Loma Naval Base in San Diego, California.

Gary breathed in a deep breath of fresh, salty, coastal air. It was good to breathe outdoor air after months of manufactured oxygen occasionally mixed with the smell of someone's dirty socks. Even the smell of car fumes as he got closer to the road was welcome and comforting.

Gary paused and looked around at the palm trees and the blue sky. "Wow, I forgot how blue the sky actually is!" A mate who was passing by patted his shoulder in agreement.

Gary carried his large duffel bag slung over his shoulder and headed to the housing quarters on the military base.

The next day, Gary went on leave for two weeks. Before traveling home to Arizona to see his family, he stopped at the navy medical hospital.

Gary had a small backpack slung over one shoulder as he stepped out of the elevator and started looking for his friend Jason's room. When he arrived, he looked in before saying anything. The man in the hospital bed had bandages wrapped around his head and covering both of his eyes. A mass of white bandaging was wrapped thickly around a stump right below the elbow where his arm had once been. Gary stood in the doorway for a moment and took a deep breath before entering.

"Knock, knock, Jason. Are you in here?" Gary said, forcing himself to be cheerful.

"Who's there?" Jason asked. His voice was dry and gravelly.

"It's me, Gary. I heard about what happened with the explosion and everything… How are you doing? Are they taking good care of you in here?"

"Did you hear about Joey and Lawrence?" Jason asked.

Gary replied in a softer tone, "Yes, I heard about them. I'm really sorry…it's a horrible thing that happened."

After some small talk from Gary and then an awkward silence, Jason spoke again. "It was all my fault, you know. I should have been the one who died." He paused. "I didn't even get to go to their funeral—I was in here, in surgery."

Gary didn't know what to say. He took a breath and let his heart talk. "Hey, Jason…come on, man. It wasn't your fault; you can't talk like that. We all knew when we signed up and put on the uniform to serve our country that there were risks. Things happen—Joey and Lawrence knew that too. You can't blame yourself for something that wasn't your fault."

Jason didn't reply.

Forcing enthusiasm into his voice, Gary said, "You'll never guess what's in my backpack. I brought you a little present!"

Jason only grunted.

"I got it while I was at the *North Pole*," Gary said, hoping to make his friend feel curious about the gift.

"Let me guess," Jason said, his voice unintentionally bitter. "You got it from Santa Claus himself while you were visiting his workshop. Did you fly on a reindeer too?"

"No, seriously, I *was* at the North Pole," Gary said. "Our sub was doing maneuvers under the Arctic ice shelf when the captain pulled a surprise drill out of his sleeve and had us work some joint maneuvers with the Brits." Enthusiasm built in his voice as he explained the whole story about surfacing at the North Pole, meeting the crew of the HMS *Tireless,* the gift exchange, and all the exciting details.

"And then when we were all headed back on board, someone spotted a polar bear. It was huge! We watched from the deck as it came right up to the tail of our sub—it sniffed around and wasn't scared or anything. It was one of the most amazing things I've ever seen!"

"So what did the Brit sailor give you?" Jason asked curiously.

"Oh, yeah. I got so carried away with my story I almost forgot," Gary said.

He reached in his backpack and pulled out the three wise men one by one. He handed them to Jason so that he could feel them and then placed them on the window ledge next to the hospital bed.

"They'll be right here, waiting for you. So when are they going to take your bandages off and see how your eyes are doing?" Gary asked.

Jason's voice cracked as he answered. "I overheard two of the nurses talking…they thought I was asleep. They said the doctor who cleaned me up doesn't think I will be able to see again—he said it would take a miracle."

Gary reached out and put his hand on Jason's shoulder. "I don't know what's going to happen, but I want you to know I'm glad you're alive." He struggled to keep his own voice under control. "And I want you to keep fighting no matter what. You're alive for a reason."

Gary paused for a moment, then asked, "Do you mind if I pray with you?"

Jason swallowed with difficulty and cleared his throat. "Yeah, that would be all right."

As Gary was praying, Chip suddenly spoke to the other wise men.

"Do you see him?" he asked with excitement in his voice.

"See who?" came the reply from Uncle.

"The angel," Chip said.

"I don't see an angel," replied Harold and Uncle.

"Not *an* angel, *the* angel—the one from Clemons's Store. He was standing in the doorway and then he turned and walked away."

Neither Harold nor Uncle was positioned with a direct view of the doorway. They wanted to believe Chip, but they had their doubts. When the angel had appeared at Clemons's Store, just the sight of him had terrified Nick and Eddie almost to death. It was hard to believe that the same angel could just be nonchalantly standing in the doorway.

"Was he glowing? Did he have wings? What makes you think it was him?" Harold inquired.

"No, it was his face. I'm sure it was him…well, I'm pretty sure it was him, but he just looked like a normal person this time, not an angel."

"Maybe it was just a person who looked like the angel," Uncle suggested.

"Well, I don't know. Maybe it was just a person." Chip wondered if his eyes were playing tricks on him. He cleared his throat and added, "And he had a mop in his hand."

That pretty much settled it for Harold and Uncle.

"Why would an angel of the Lord, one of God's mighty warriors, be walking around with a mop in his hand?" Uncle asked Chip.

"You're right, that doesn't make any sense. I think maybe I was just seeing things," Chip said, disappointed—for he really had hoped it was the angel he had seen.

"Gruuumph, grunt!" came a noise from Thunder.

Chip answered the grunts. "Thank you for believing in me, Thunder, but I think I was just mistaken."

The wise men were silent as their attention was drawn back to the two men in the hospital room. They listened to them talk some more before Gary said good-bye and left. The wise men were growing more and more concerned about the injured man. Though Gary had tried his best to boost Jason's spirits by giving him some hopeful words of encouragement, Jason's heart was revealed in the things he said. He blamed himself for his friends' deaths; he said he should have died instead of them. At one point, he even said he wished he were dead. All of his dreams were over; he felt useless with only one arm and no eyesight.

The mission of the three wise men was clear. Here before them was a man who was in great emotional, physical, and spiritual pain—a man who desperately needed hope.

But there was a problem. Jason was not a crying baby or even a blue-eyed orphan child. Harold, Chip, and Uncle felt unprepared for the task. They discussed every sermon they had ever heard; they reminisced about conversations they had heard Father Andrew and Scottie having with the children over the years of their short existence. It would take all their understanding of human nature to help this young man!

Chip was still struggling with whether he had actually seen the angel earlier in the day. Gary had gone, and other than a nurse coming in to check his vital signs every half hour or so, Jason was alone. He drifted in and out of sleep. The pain medicine made his head cloudy.

The days leading up to Christmas Eve were a time for the wise men to listen to and observe every interaction and conversation Jason had so they could get to know him better. No family came to visit him, but they learned a lot just from his conversations with the nurses. He had been in foster care most of his childhood. He hadn't gotten along very well with his last foster family and had been all too happy to join the military as soon as he was eligible. He considered his only family to be the other men in his unit, along with a few friends from high school, and now he was dealing with the fact that two of his buddies, who were like brothers to him, were dead, and he felt responsible.

The three wise men discussed their plan. They decided that they would break one of their rules and talk to Jason. Because his eyes were bandaged, they reasoned that they could talk to him without him realizing who or what they really were. When they had learned about Jason's life, they felt that they *did* know how to relate to him and his situation. Their time at the orphanage had given them firsthand experience with the type of loneliness and hopelessness Jason had experienced. His physical injuries were serious, to be sure, but his heart was most in need of hope and healing.

December 23rd came, and Jason spent many of the daytime hours sleeping. The hospital appeared to be running with a skeleton crew, and the nurses seemed in a bigger hurry to get their tasks done than usual. Midnight came.

Jason was awake, sitting up in bed, and hoping that maybe one of the nurses would have a little time to talk. He was bored. He really wished he could just sit and watch TV, but he didn't even want it on if he couldn't see it.

From the windowsill, Harold was the first to speak. "Hello. I see you are awake."

Jason sat up and turned his head toward the voice. "Hello—you startled me! I didn't hear you come in. Are you a new nurse?"

"No, my name is Harold. I'm here with two of my friends, Chip and Uncle."

"Hi," said Chip.

"Hello," said Uncle.

"We just wanted to take some time to visit with you and keep you company for a while, if that is okay," Harold explained.

"Yeah, that's fine—I was just sitting here bored anyway." Jason sat up a little straighter. "What time is it, anyway?"

"It's a little after midnight," Harold answered.

Jason whistled. "Boy, you guys are out late. But hey, I'm glad to have someone to talk to."

While the wise men got acquainted with Jason, Thunder just stayed hunkered down, listening. Chip kept glancing at Thunder to see if he would go off exploring the way he normally did, but every time he looked, Thunder was sitting in the same position with his feet tucked under him. After a while, Chip and Uncle hopped down and moved to the other side of the room, perching themselves on the back of a small vinyl chair where they continued talking. Harold remained on the windowsill. The wise men were so engrossed in their conversation with Jason that they didn't notice when someone walking by the doorway attracted the camel's attention. Without notice, Thunder was up and disappeared, trotting down the hall.

The hall was a corridor of sterile white tile with high gloss wax that reflected the florescent lights that stretched the length of the ceiling in each direction. Thunder slowed to a walk and looked left, then right. To the left, a nurse came out of a patient's room and walked the opposite direction down the long hallway. To the right, someone else was walking away. The stranger turned the corner into another hallway. Thunder followed.

The hospital was quiet and still. When Thunder neared the corner, he could see that the two hallways met at an intersection. He turned right, searching for the figure he had seen walk by the door. The hall was empty, but he could hear voices coming from an open area ahead.

Thunder lumbered down the hall toward the voices. The white-tiled floor turned into carpet and opened into a waiting area furnished with upholstered chairs and couches, end tables that were piled with magazines, and a sampling of plastic plants and trees in brass pots. Thunder quickly slipped behind a couch and out the other side, where he stopped and peeked around the brass pot of a fake broad-leafed plant.

Several feet up the hall from the sitting area, a nurse was talking to two women at a nurses' station. Across from the plant, a little girl around five years old was asleep on a couch, clinging to a bright, multicolored blanket.

The little girl's eyes opened and blinked a few times as she remembered where she was. When her eyes adjusted, she found herself looking directly at Thunder, who was a short distance across the room. But Thunder did not see the little girl's eyes open, and he was already moving to hide behind a chair a few feet away.

The little girl sat up. "Mommy, can I play with the baby camel?"

One of the women turned to the little girl. "Oh, Abigail, you're awake. What did you say, sweetie?"

Back in Jason's room, Harold, Chip, and Uncle were still talking with Jason.

"I never really thought of it that way before," Jason said. "But you are right; being in foster care is a lot like being an orphan. Even though I lived with a family, I never felt like it was a *real* family. I always held back. I didn't want to get too close because I knew I could be moved at any time without warning." Jason stroked and smoothed at his bed sheet as he talked. He really didn't know why he was being so open with these strangers—maybe because it was so late at night.

"So did you guys work at this orphanage...are you like clergy or something?" Jason asked.

Uncle spoke up. "We like to think of ourselves as servants of God, but we are not clergy."

Jason scratched his head. "I'm not a religious person—sometimes religious people make me a little uncomfortable—but you guys are really easy to talk to." He frowned, but it wasn't an unhappy frown. "There is something different about you." As soon as he said that, something inside him felt the need to put up a defensive wall, perhaps out of habit.

"I don't have anything against religion or anything; you know, whatever makes you happy. All truth is relative anyway."

Harold's eyebrow shot up in analysis of Jason's statement.

"The statement 'All truth is relative' states an absolute, so if it is true, it must be absolutely true. If it is absolutely true, then not all things are relative, and the statement that 'All truth is relative' is false." Harold delivered this observation in a truly analytical tone, as only he could do. He did not sound the least bit defensive or argumentative, and the effect of his words could be seen on Jason's face as he thought about what Harold had said. Slowly he let the corner of his mouth curl into a slight smile.

Uncle and Chip looked at each other, stunned by Harold's pure logic.

Just then, Chip looked around and thought, *Where did Thunder go?*

"Can I play with the baby camel, Mommy?" Abigail repeated, pointing across the room at the couch.

Thunder's eyes opened wide. He stayed out of sight behind the couch.

"Oh, sweetheart, you must have been dreaming." Her mother sat down next to Abigail and gave her a hug. "Listen, Grandma and I were just talking to the nurse, and she said that Grandpa came through his heart surgery just fine. The heart attack didn't cause much damage because he got help so quickly. The doctor is going to come out and talk to us in a little while."

"Is Grandpa going to be okay, Mama?" Abigail asked.

"He's in great hands, and I think he will pull through this just fine. We will find out more after we talk to the doctor." The mother snuggled her little girl close and rested her chin on her head. "We will just have to keep praying for him, okay?"

Thunder stayed hidden behind the couch until he saw the mother and the grandma walk down the hall to talk to the doctor. Then, slowly, he poked his head out to see where the little girl was…

"Hello, little camel," said Abigail, her nose almost touching Thunder's. She was on her hands and knees, peeking around the couch.

Thunder stood still, but Abigail reached around, picked him up, and took him back to the couch with her. She looked down the long hallway to the nurse's station and waved at her mom, who was listening to the doctor. Her mom waved back. To Abigail's right, and down another hallway, the mother could see a hospital janitor sweeping and gradually moving in their direction.

Abigail started petting Thunder while she talked, and he couldn't help but enjoy it. He let out a little grunt of pleasure and smiled at her with his big brown eyes.

"That's my mom and grandma down there…they're talking to the doctor. Grandpa is a mil-i-tar-y chap-lain." Abigail broke the bigger words into syllables as she talked. She kept petting Thunder as she talked. "My grandpa is sick. I hope he is going to be okay."

She patted him on the head and said, "You're a nice little camel. I like you."

"His name is Thunder," came a strong, friendly voice from beside her on the couch.

Abigail looked up and saw the hospital janitor standing at the edge of the carpet, leaning against his cleaning cart and smiling. He was a tall, strong-looking man with long, straight dark hair. He had dark brown eyes, almond skin, and chiseled features. His face reminded Abigail of one of the American Indian greeting cards she had seen in the gift shop earlier. She instinctively felt warm and at ease with this stranger, when normally she would have been bashful.

"Is he your camel?" she asked, smiling back at the janitor.

"No, but I know who he belongs to," came the reply.

Abigail could see past the man to where her mom and grandma were still talking to the doctor. Her mom put her arm around Grandma. It looked as if Grandma was crying.

The janitor followed Abigail's gaze and then looked back at Abigail again. "They're talking about your grandpa, aren't they?" he said tenderly.

"Yeah," Abigail said, still stroking Thunder's fur. "I hope Papa is going to be okay."

The janitor moved closer and sat on the arm of the couch. "I can tell you that no matter what happens with your grandpa, he *will* be okay. Even if he dies he will be okay, because he is friends with God, and he is one of God's children—just like you are, Abigail."

Abigail smiled. It did not seem strange to her that this man talked to her about the possibility of her grandpa dying. She had already thought about that, even though the grownups hadn't said anything about death when they had told her about Grandpa's heart attack.

"You know my name," Abigail said as she studied the janitor's face, trying to remember if she had met him before.

"Yes, Abigail is a beautiful name. It comes from the Hebrew language and means *joy of the Father*," said the man.

"Do you know my grandpa?" she asked.

"Yes, I know him very well. He has helped many people over the years; he is a good and faithful servant," the janitor replied.

"My grandpa's favorite Bible verse is John 3:16: 'For God so loved the world that he gave his only begotten son so that whoever believes in him will not die but have everlasting life.' Grandpa helped me learn that," Abigail said proudly.

The little girl looked intently into the face of the man and said, "Can you ask God to please make my grandpa better? I don't want him to go to heaven yet."

The janitor's face showed sincere love and compassion. "The Lord has heard the words you just said, and he knows the very desires of your heart. Always remember that you can talk to God yourself at any time, and he will listen."

"I know, but will you ask him for me anyway?" Abigail asked, and then she yawned, her whole face overtaken by sleepiness she couldn't hold back.

"I will ask," the janitor replied.

Abigail looked down at Thunder as her head drooped a bit and her eyes grew heavy.

The man gently placed his hand on Abigail's shoulder. "You're a tired girl. Why don't you lie back down and get some rest? I need to take Thunder with me."

Thunder gave Abigail a final loving nudge with his head, then bounded over the soft cushion to the man, who picked him up and placed him on the cleaning cart. Abigail lay down on the couch, and the man covered her with her blanket.

The janitor went to his cart and pointed it toward the hall where Jason's room was located.

"Do you have a favorite Bible verse?" Abigail asked as she raised herself up on one elbow.

The janitor turned back to her with a smile.

"I have many favorites, but here is one for you to look up later: Hebrews 13:2."

"I hope I don't forget it," Abigail said sleepily.

"You won't," the man said as he walked away, pushing his cart.

As the janitor turned the corner and disappeared out of sight, Abigail's mom and grandma came back to the sitting area. Her mom sat next to her on the couch and started stroking her hair. Abigail leaned against her, her eyes closing in the comfort she felt being with her mom.

"What did you and that man talk about, sweetie?"

"Grandpa...and the camel," Abigail replied sleepily.

"Who was he? Did you ask his name?" Mom asked.

"I forgot to...but he is an angel," Abigail said with closed eyes. Smiling, she drifted off to sleep.

Mom and Grandma just looked at each other and shrugged their shoulders.

"Children say the cutest things," Grandma said with a smile.

Thunder looked into Jason's room from the hall. He spied Chip sitting on the back of a blue vinyl chair next to Uncle with their legs dangling in front of them. Thunder crossed the floor, hopped up on the chair, and lay down below Chip's feet. Chip slid down next to the camel.

"Where have you been?" Chip whispered.

Thunder grunted several syllables in low tones.

"The angel *was* here?" Chip whispered in response.

Jason, who had been talking to Harold, turned in Chip's direction. "Was that somebody's stomach I heard growling?"

"Oh, yes, I, ah, I guess that was me," said Chip.

Just then, the overnight nurse walked briskly into the room to check Jason's vital signs.

Harold, Chip, and Uncle remained still and quiet.

"You're up awful late," the nurse said, looking at a chart in her hand. "Is your pain medicine working okay?"

"Yeah, I think I slept most of the day—I'm just not tired," Jason replied. "Besides, having company sure makes the passing of time more enjoyable."

The nurse checked a few things off as she bustled around. "Yeah, having someone to talk to is a good thing—I wish I could stay longer and talk with you, but we are real short-staffed tonight." She checked Jason's bandages and blood pressure, temperature, and pulse.

"Well, I'll be fine sitting here just talking to my new friends," Jason replied.

The nurse chuckled. "Well, you and your *friends* keep it down in here. Some people are sleeping, you know." She chuckled again. "I'll be back to check on you later." Then she headed out the door.

Jason talked with his new friends all night. They discussed the meaning and purpose of life. They discussed faith, God, and family, and Jason even opened up about the explosion and the death of his friends. The discussions went from laughter to tears, from serious reflection to simple pondering. Jason thought that he had never talked so much or so openly in his life. He usually kept things bottled up. But these guys made him feel so at ease. There was a simple, almost childlike innocence about each of them. Yet, they spoke with a certainty and clarity of purpose that he had never come across before.

Growing up in foster care had caused Jason to be cautious of new relationships, and that same wariness transferred to people he had met in the various churches he had attended in his life. When he was ten years old, he'd had a foster dad who thought he knew everything that was best for Jason. The trouble was that he never took the time to hear what Jason needed, wanted, or even liked. The foster dad took it for granted that every ten-year-old boy must love football. Jason got a football jersey from the foster dad's favorite team as a birthday present; he got dragged to every local high school and college football game; his life became all about football. He might have had a passing interest in football when he arrived at that home, but his foster dad actually taught him how to hate it. He was glad that he'd only had to spend one year trapped in that home.

As he told the wise men, Jason had met people in church who reminded him of his football dad. They seemed more interested in telling him what he needed, or assuming what he believed instead of actually getting to know him. He had given up on religion a long time ago, but the more he talked to these three men, who so obviously believed in God, the more he started thinking—not of religion, but of God, and if there really was a God who cared about him. He could tell that Harold, Chip, and Uncle truly cared. They were not trying to win a point or make him feel guilty like so many church people in his life had done. They were genuine.

The time passed quickly, and it was getting close to dawn, but the conversation wasn't over yet.

"Why," Harold was saying, "I once doubted whether I had any purpose in my life at all!"

Jason was quiet for a moment, but there was urgency in his voice when he asked, "What do you mean by that?"

Harold answered with his usual logic. "There was a point when I reasoned that perhaps I was stuck in an uncomfortable position because I was being punished for something I didn't even know I had done. I thought that maybe I had no purpose in life except to sit around be miserable and do nothing. Just to put my life on a shelf, so to speak, and do nothing, hope for nothing, just exist—trapped in a shell of a body."

"That's exactly how I have been feeling," Jason said with a deep sigh. Then the urgency came back. "What changed? I mean, you seem so sure of yourself now."

"It is difficult to explain, but God revealed himself to me in a very dramatic way."

"He revealed himself to all of us," Chip added.

"God gave us a purpose—that is, he called us to a purpose higher than ourselves," Uncle explained.

Jason was silent, deep in thought for a moment. "What is your purpose? And what can *my* purpose be? What could God possibly do with a one-armed blind guy?"

Harold spoke up again. "Only God can reveal your purpose to you. But if you don't look for it, you risk missing it altogether. As for us and our purpose in life, it is to travel wherever the Lord happens to bring us so that we can help people…people like you, Jason."

Chip, Uncle, and Thunder moved back to their positions on the windowsill while Jason sat quietly reflecting on the entire night of conversation.

"Jason," Uncle spoke up, "it's almost daylight, and we have to get going. Thank you for talking with us. We will remember this night always."

"Wow, it's almost morning? We've been talking all night! You guys can come back, though, right?"

Chip answered, "No…I'm sorry, but we are leaving—on to the next mission and place that only God knows."

"Do you think God would ever reveal himself to me—you know, give me a sign or something?" Jason asked.

At that moment, the nurse walked into the room. "I'm here to do one final check. I have to go cover another station for a few hours, but someone else will check on you."

The nurse chatted as she went about doing her routine checks. "It's been an interesting morning so far—our chaplain, who works here at the hospital, had a heart attack last night. The doctors thought he was a goner—they had to do open-heart surgery to unblock his arteries."

The nurse paused as she wrote on the chart.

"Anyway, he wakes up this morning and tells his nurse that an angel came to him and told him that God still had a purpose for him here on earth. He's convinced that he really saw an angel and that it wasn't some hallucination."

She paused again as she started changing one of the IV drip bags. "But get this! The granddaughter who was here at the hospital last night says she also saw *and talked to* an angel, and he looked just like the angel her grandpa described." She made another notation on the medical chart and jabbed the air with her pen. "But it gets better! The mom and the grandma saw their granddaughter talking to a man; they thought he was a custodian, but the granddaughter says she knows he was an angel."

The nurse paused for effect and softened her voice. "The weird thing is that we don't have any custodians that match this man's description. All of our cleaning crew are women, and they were all in the break room when this supposedly happened. And the *real* strange thing? Our security cameras don't show any trace of this guy—whoever he was!"

"Wow, that's strange," Jason said. He chuckled. "You guys were here all night talking with me. Did you see any angels walking around?"

There was a momentary silence.

"Who are you talking to?" asked the nurse as the first rays of morning light gleamed through the window.

Jason frowned. "Uncle, Harold, and Chip; I assumed you knew them—I mean, since they were allowed to be in here all night."

"Jason, there is nobody here...I've worked all night, and there has not been anyone in your room but me."

"But—but they were just here. We were talking when you walked in the room. Come on, guys, don't tease me like this—this isn't funny." Jason swept his arm toward the window. "They were just here...they were talking when you walked in the room. You had to see them!"

"Jason! I'm serious. There is nobody here."

As Jason sat up straighter, he reached his arm toward the window, feeling for his friends. And even as he did, he noticed something—something new. He could see something white—no...it was *light* penetrating through his bandages. Jason reached up and started pulling the tape and bandages away from his eyes. The nurse protested, but it was too late. Off came the bandages. Gauze fell to the floor.

Jason blinked hard several times as the tears began to flow. He saw three blurred figures silhouetted by the light streaming in through the window. For a moment, he was relieved to see that his friends were actually there in the room with him. But then his eyes came into focus, and he could see it was just the Christmas decorations on the windowsill with the morning light shining behind them. He looked around the room and back at the nurse. Emotion welled up in him, and he let go with sobbing tears. "I can see, I can see!"

Chapter Eleven

FOLLOW MY VOICE

After their Christmas at the hospital, the wise men changed hands again. After his release from the hospital, Jason traveled east to visit a friend and decided to donate the small statues to a secondhand store. Eventually the trio and their camel ended up in the home of a retired couple in Nashville, Tennessee. Over the next few years, the wise men and the camel witnessed the couple grow older together with each passing year. The experience was a stark contrast to the time they had spent observing the activities of the orphanage. They learned even more about the human characteristics of love, devotion, tenderness, and kindness. Each Christmas, with its twelve days of observation and one night of life and activity, came and went without any dramatic rescues or interventions on the part of the wise men. They began to wonder if they had been sent to this home to retire, like their hosts.

Without realizing it, the wise men also increased their knowledge of the world outside of Mr. and Mrs. Miller's home. Mr. Miller had a habit of falling asleep in his easy chair while watching the news. The wise men

were often amazed and shocked at what they learned while watching television from their place atop the fireplace mantel.

Then came the Christmas when Mrs. Miller was home alone; Mr. Miller had passed away. Mrs. Miller received visits from friends who stopped by to check on her. She showed strength and courage in the presence of her visitors as she faced her first Christmas alone, but behind closed doors, the wise men saw her slumped posture and heard her sobs as she sat in the living room staring at Mr. Miller's empty chair.

A couple more Christmases passed before Chip, Harold, Uncle, and Thunder found themselves in the small, tidy nursing-home room of Mrs. Miller. They spent several Christmases at the nursing home and had some interesting adventures too—but those stories are for another time. More importantly, during their time at the nursing home, they became acquainted with the next family they would come to know and care for.

Pastor Dwayne Jones and his family made regular weekly visits to the nursing home where Mrs. Miller lived. He and his wife, Anita, and three children, Isaiah, Sophie, and Faith, were regular faces at the nursing home, and they truly enjoyed the time they spent there with their friends.

Pastor Dwayne Jones went by the nickname of Pastor DJ. People were always telling him he had the strong, rhythmical voice of a radio personality, so DJ seemed to fit him perfectly. He was the son of a pastor; in fact, he was the fourth-generation pastor in his family.

Pastor DJ's great-grandfather and grandmother had been slaves who managed to escape to freedom on the Underground Railroad. Great-Grandpa Isaiah had possessed a clear calling from God. After starting a new life in the North, he began meeting with community members under an old oak tree to have Bible study and preach the Word of God. Even during the week, after long hours of backbreaking work, he and his wife would spend their evenings teaching black neighbors and friends how to read and write. On Sundays, they would study the Word of God and sing hymns. People would come from miles around just to sit under that old oak and hear Isaiah speak in his strong, resonating voice. Carrying on the family legacy, Pastor DJ was the pastor at the Old Oak Baptist Church in the suburbs of Nashville, where his spirited sermons were an inspiration to all who heard them.

Harold, Chip, and Uncle liked Pastor DJ immediately. Though he had his own unique personality, they agreed that his inner spirit reminded them of Father Andrew and Scottie. In fact, the entire Jones family had a genuine spirit that drew the wise men. Isaiah, their oldest, was sixteen when the wise men first met him. He would come on his own after school to visit and sometimes read to the elderly residents whose eyes weren't as good as they used to be. He became especially good friends with Mrs. Miller and considered her a grandmother to him.

Once when Isaiah was eighteen years old, he brought a friend with him to visit Mrs. Miller. It was on December 14th in the afternoon.

"Hello, Mrs. Miller. How are you doing today?" Isaiah asked after gently knocking on the doorframe to her room.

Mrs. Miller's face lit up. "Why, Isaiah! It is so good to see you. Come in, come in and sit a spell."

"I brought a friend with me today. I hope you don't mind," Isaiah said as he motioned to someone in the hall to follow him.

"Oh, it's no bother at all. I would love to meet one of your friends," Mrs. Miller said.

A young man, the same age as Isaiah, walked into the room. He was dressed neatly and had sandy blond hair and blue eyes. He stretched out his hand to Mrs. Miller. "Hello, ma'am, I'm JW. It's nice to meet you."

Mrs. Miller shook his hand with a gentle squeeze and said, "It's nice to meet you too. It's so nice to meet young people who still know how to say a proper greeting." Mrs. Miller cupped her other hand on top of JW's as she continued to shake his hand gently. "You know, young folks just don't seem to know how to shake hands these days, and they certainly don't say ma'am or sir very often."

JW smiled and blushed a little. "Yes, ma'am, I think I know what you mean."

Mrs. Miller motioned for the two boys to have a seat.

"Did you hear that?" Uncle said.

"I sure did," replied Chip. "He said his name is JW. You don't suppose . . .?"

Harold spoke up. "I'm sure there are many JWs in the world. Besides, we're half a world away from the JW we knew. Statistically speaking, it is very unlikely that this is the same JW from the orphanage."

Uncle was figuring out loud. "Let's see...five plus twelve, no wait, thirteen Christmases...yes, he certainly appears to be the right age."

"Say, is that a bit of an English accent I notice?" asked Mrs. Miller.

"It sure is," JW answered with a smile. "I lived in London until I was five. My mom is British and my dad is American."

"I see! So how long have you boys known each other?"

117

"JW and I have been friends for a few years," Isaiah said. "His dad and my dad are old friends. When JW and his parents moved to Nashville, they started coming to our church." Isaiah looked at JW and smiled a mischievous smile. "I think poor JW here was terrified the first time."

JW quirked a smile. "Maybe I was a little scared of this guy," he said, pointing his thumb at Isaiah, "but not of the church. It was just different from what I was used to—that's all."

"Oh, is that so," said Mrs. Miller, smiling at both of them.

"Well, you know how carried away my dad gets when he's on a roll." Isaiah was chuckling as he talked. "And with all the shouts of 'Amen!' and 'You go, Pastor!' and the 'Uh-huhs' and 'Alrights'…" He chuckled again. "I think poor JW here thought he had stepped onto another planet or something."

JW chuckled along with his friend. "It was certainly a lot less reserved than the type of church I was used to."

Isaiah added, "Not to mention that you used to be pretty shy when you were younger."

"Oh, you boys are so much fun," Mrs. Miller said. She reached over and patted JW's knee. "You're not the only one who has had that experience. Where I grew up, I never had the opportunity to go to a black church either."

Mrs. Miller put her hand up to her mouth and looked at Isaiah. "Oh, I'm sorry. Is it okay to say…black church?"

Isaiah smiled. "Mrs. Miller, you're fine. There's nothin' wrong with stating the obvious. We consider our church to be of the black church tradition, even though we have a mix of all kinds of people in our church family."

Mrs. Miller's blush faded. "Oh, I'm glad I didn't say anything wrong."

Isaiah placed his hand on Mrs. Miller's shoulder and smiled. "Ma'am, you're so sweet, I don't think you could offend anyone even if you tried."

Mrs. Miller smiled and turned her attention back to JW. "I had an uncle that went by JW. James William was his name. Are you a James William also?"

JW scratched his head. "Well, I just go by JW—I don't really know if it's short for anything." He smiled apologetically at the puzzled look on Mrs. Miller's face. "Well, you see, I was dropped off at an orphanage when I was just a baby. I don't know who my biological mother is. Anyway, there was a note pinned on my blanket that said 'please take care of JW'…so that's my name."

"Holy star of Bethlehem, did you hear that!" Harold exclaimed. "I just knew it had to be *our* JW!"

Mrs. Miller had a nice long visit with the two boys. She asked about JW's adoption and family and talked about her own childhood. From the conversation, the wise men learned what had happened after they left England: Elizabeth had accepted Hiram's marriage proposal, and she had told him the heartbreaking story of how a little boy named JW just wanted a family for Christmas. They had made the decision to get married and to adopt JW. Then they moved to the United States and started their new life together.

As the boys were saying good-bye, JW looked up and for the first time noticed the three wise men and the camel sitting on the small nightstand, half-hidden behind a large poinsettia.

"Oh my gosh! These look just like…" JW paused. He reached down, picked up Chip and Thunder, and rolled them over in his hands, inspecting them. "There's a chip in his robe," JW said in disbelief.

"What are you talking about?" Isaiah asked.

"The orphanage had some figurines just like this—I remember playing with them one time…and pretending that they were real and could talk to me." JW chuckled and set the ceramic piece back down.

"I must have had a pretty good imagination. It still seems so real to me, though, even today." JW turned back to his friend and finished saying goodbye to Mrs. Miller. Then they left.

Another Christmas came and went at the nursing home. The following year, when the wise men came to life on December 12th, they had changed locations once more.

"We are in a new place again," Chip noted when their senses returned to them.

The months of slumber they experienced between Christmases often found them wrapped in tissue paper and packed away in boxes in storage closets or attics. As such, they were protected and well preserved. Their paint still held its original luster, and except for the damage to Chip's robe, they showed no signs of wear.

"We sure have moved around a lot since our time at the orphanage. I wonder who lives in this house," Uncle said.

Just then, a little girl around four years old walked into the room carrying a small blue plastic bowl in her hand. The tight, dark curls of her hair were pulled into two pigtails, which were held in place on each side of her head by white and pink beads.

A woman's voice called from the other room, "Faith, where are you going with those Cheerios?"

"I want to watch TV, Momma," Faith called over her shoulder as she sat in the middle of the living room and looked at the blank screen. "Can you turn the TV on for me?"

The mother came walking into the room, stopped, stood with her hands on her hips and looked at Faith with a frown on her face.

"Sweetheart, Mommy just got done vacuuming in here, and you watched TV earlier anyway. Please take your snack back to the kitchen table, and I'll find a book for you to look at while I finish cleaning the house. Daddy invited some guests to come over tonight, and I still need to clean the bathroom and tidy up the kitchen…oh, and I still have laundry to do."

Faith looked up and blinked innocently. "You could have just said 'No'—it wouldn't have taken so long."

"I recognize the mom!" said Harold. "That's Anita Jones, the pastor's wife."

"Oh, they seem like such a nice family," Chip mused.

Pastor DJ's home was bustling with activity. Their kids' friends seemed to think of it as their second home. Someone was always being invited to dinner, and Anita and Pastor DJ worked as a wonderful team as they shared the love of Christ in tangible ways. The idea of sharing a cup of water in the name of Christ was not lost on them. They shared their home, their meals, and the love of their family with anyone and everyone they came into contact with.

As the wise men got to know the Jones family better, their excitement grew as they wondered what mission they might be called upon to complete for this energetic family.

"Mom! Where's my karate uniform?" Isaiah yelled as he bopped down the stairs of the multilevel home.

"Did you look in the dryer? I washed all the karate uniforms last night," Anita yelled back from the kitchen.

The wise men had pieced together several conversations and figured out that not only was Pastor DJ a pastor, but he was also a martial arts instructor.

Pastor DJ taught karate at his church building in the fellowship hall. People who would otherwise never set foot in a church would come into Sensei Jones's karate class on Mondays, Wednesdays, and Thursdays. Pastor DJ had started training in martial arts when he was fifteen. His karate instructor had been a very influential mentor in his life and had shown him how living the way of the warrior was an analogy for living the way of Christ.

"Was your uniform in the dryer?" Anita asked Isaiah as she walked out of the kitchen.

"Yeah, Mom. I have to get there early because Dad wants me to get class started for him. He has some meeting that's going to make him a little late." Isaiah carried a laundry basket of clean clothes out from the laundry room.

"I don't know what your daddy's going to do when you move off to college," Anita said, reaching for the laundry basket. "Here, let me take those—you better grab your uniform and get going."

"Thanks, Mom!" Isaiah gave his mom a kiss, ran up the stairs to grab his bag, and flew out the door.

"I sure like that young man," said Harold. "I wonder what mission God will have for us this Christmas. This family seems to be doing so well; I wonder how we might be able to help them?"

"Well, I have faith that God will reveal it to us when the time is right," said Uncle.

"I do too," said Harold, adding, "Though it is hard to wait sometimes."

Chip spoke up. "I'm just wondering what kind of mischief Thunder might get into this Christmas."

"Gruumph!" came the response from Thunder.

"Just seeing if you were listening, my hairy friend," Chip added with a chuckle.

Several days passed, and on December 22nd, the wise men got a pleasant surprise.

The Jones family had just finished dinner when there was a knock at the door.

"I'll get it!" yelled Sophie. They heard her voice as she opened the door. "Hey, JW! Come on in." Sophie yelled over her shoulder, "Isaiah! You've got company!"

JW walked into the living room wearing a dark blue winter coat pulled up tight around his neck. He kept his coat zipped tight and his hands in his pockets.

"He looks cold. It's hard to believe he is the little baby left out on a cold London night so many years ago," Chip commented from his vantage point on the mantelpiece.

"He looks uptight, like there's something wrong," Uncle said.

Isaiah came into the room. "Hey, JW. Sorry to keep you waiting. I was just finishing drying some dishes for Mom. It's good to see you! How's it going?"

JW hesitated and looked around the room. "Uh, well, I'm not sure. I mean, well, I need to talk to you." JW's hands came out of his pockets, and he stroked his hair back and let his hand rest on the back of his neck for a moment. "Do you think I can talk to you and your dad together?"

"Yeah, sure, man. Whatever you need, we're here for you; you know that." Isaiah put his hand on his friend's shoulder. "Have a seat. Hey, Dad!" called Isaiah.

Pastor DJ walked into the room with his normal upbeat smile. "Hey guys!"

"Dad, JW needs to talk to us. You got a minute?" said Isaiah.

"Of course," Pastor DJ replied. He took a seat in the chair across from where JW was sitting on the couch and leaned forward, giving his undivided attention to their guest.

JW loosened up a bit and unzipped his coat. He looked back and forth from Isaiah to Pastor DJ.

"I've been doing a lot of thinking the past couple of months, and I've decided I'm not going back to school after Christmas break."

Isaiah couldn't hold in his astonishment. "But we were going to be roommates! That's just a couple of weeks away—we had it all planned."

Pastor DJ shot a glance at Isaiah and said, "Hold on, son. Let's hear him out."

Isaiah's face softened. "I'm sorry about that. Go on."

JW slumped forward with his elbows on his knees and stared at his hands as he wrung them together.

"After the accident…after losing my mom and dad…things just haven't been the same. I'm not the same. School…well, school just doesn't seem important to me anymore." JW's voice cracked as he held back his emotion.

Pastor DJ and Isaiah looked at each other, deep empathy in their faces.

On the mantelpiece, the wise men gasped in shock.

Pastor DJ got up and sat next to JW on the couch, putting his arm around JW's shoulder.

"I think I know how you feel. I lost my mom when I was young too. It's a feeling I still haven't quite gotten over. Losing a parent…it changes you."

JW's hands came up to his face for a moment. His voice trembled with emotion. "I didn't want to come here and cry tonight. It's been eight months since Mom and Dad died in that car crash. I just wanted to tell you guys my plans…you're really the only family I have now."

Harold, Chip, and Uncle were stunned.

"Elizabeth…Elizabeth is dead," Chip said slowly as if he could not believe his own words.

JW sniffed a couple of times and blotted his wet eyes with his sleeve.

"Anyway, what I wanted to come and tell you first—Isaiah, I'm really sorry that I'm bailing on you, man. I know you can find another roommate easily—you're one of the easiest people to get along with that I know."

Isaiah nodded and said, "Thanks. And yeah, I can probably find someone else to help share the rent, but it won't be the same as rooming with my best friend, though." He cleared his throat, more careful this time not to trample on his friend's feelings. "If you're not going back to college, what are you going to do? Where are you going to go?"

JW looked up. "I've given this a lot of thought, and I've made up my mind. I'm going to London to visit the orphanage where my mom and dad adopted me."

Pastor DJ nodded with a smile, and JW continued.

"After I visit London, I want to travel to Uganda, where my mom and dad met. And then I want to travel and see some of the other places they told me about. I want to travel the world and go the places they went and see the things they saw."

JW sighed and leaned back into the couch. "I just can't do the school thing anymore. I thought I could carry on after the funeral and every-thing and pour my energy and grief into my studies—but it just isn't working that way."

Pastor DJ let out a thoughtful sigh and said, "Well, it sounds like you've made up your mind. All I can do is respect that and support you in your decision. And you know, I think a trip like that might do you some good—help you find your focus again." Pastor DJ gently squeezed JW's shoulder. "Is there anything we can do to help you?"

"Yeah, whatever you need, just ask," Isaiah added.

JW smiled. "Thanks," he said, letting some of the tension leave his neck and shoulders. "I've got the money from Dad's life insurance policy. The realtor called this week and told me their house is sold—so I'll get a little more money from that after the mortgage is paid off. I have my passport, and I've already talked to the school about my change in plans. Pastor DJ, I was hoping you could help me make contacts with people in some of the places I want to go."

Pastor DJ nodded. "Sure, sure, I can do that," he said. "As you know, your dad and I were in Uganda together on that mission trip when he met your mother. I can get you the names and numbers of the folks who run the mission there and help you set up a plan."

"Thanks for your help."

Pastor DJ rubbed his chin. "Now, about the orphanage in London—I don't know a whole lot about them, but I can sure help you do some of the research and make some phone calls for you."

"Me too, man. Whatever will help," Isaiah said.

The wise men too wanted to help JW in any way they could. Maybe this was their mission—to help him find some of the answers he was looking for.

Christmas Eve came, and Thunder and the wise men came to life as usual. They made their way down from the mantel and onto the living room floor.

"Okay, here's the plan. We need to find some paper and something to write with," Harold said.

Chip spoke up. "So after we write down the orphanage's address and phone number and the names of people to contact, where are we going to leave the paper so that it doesn't look too suspicious?"

"Thunder, where are you going?" Uncle said. The other wise men turned to see Thunder galloping off, sniffing the air to the left and the right.

"Maybe he's sniffing out some paper for us," said Chip.

"Well, we had better follow him. I always get nervous when he runs off like that," said Harold.

The three wise men ran after Thunder as he headed into the kitchen.

"Boy, it's foggy in here," said Chip as they entered the kitchen.

"That's not fog, it's smoke!" yelled Uncle.

Smoke was coming in blue wisps from under the door where the garage connected to the kitchen.

"Change in plans, fellas! I think we are here to put out at fire!" yelled Harold as they reached the door to the garage.

"Look!" pointed Chip. "If I can get up on the kitchen counter, I can reach the doorknob and we can get in there. What are we going to put the fire out with?"

Boom! Gas fumes caught fire, and the lawn mower gas can in the garage exploded. Flames shot everywhere. And the kitchen door blew off its hinges.

Thunder was just quick enough to knock the three wise men out of the way before the door exploded into the kitchen with shards of wood flying everywhere. Fire burst through behind it. The house rapidly filled with thick black smoke, and yellow flames crawled up the wall and onto the ceiling.

"The family! We've got to get the family out!" yelled Uncle.

They raced out of the kitchen and up the stairs. The smoke grew thicker as they moved up the stairs, and they waved it aside with their arms.

"Don't breathe it in!" Harold ordered.

"It's okay!" Chip answered. "It's not affecting us!"

As they reached the top of the stairs, they could hear Pastor DJ and his wife coughing and yelling their kids' names. Faith's room was the first one at the top of the stairs on the left. Chip and Thunder could hear her coughing and crying.

"We'll get her," Chip yelled as they entered her room. Flames were already creeping up her walls.

Harold and Uncle headed down the hall toward the other voices.

"Dad!" came Isaiah's voice.

"Mom! Dad!" called Sophie.

"Here we are!" cried Pastor DJ as he stumbled into the hallway, coughing through the shirt over his face.

Anita, Pastor DJ, and the two older kids met in the hall on their hands and knees just as Uncle and Harold reached them.

"Lord Jesus! Where's Faith? Where's my baby?" cried Anita.

Harold yelled in his deep, clear voice, "Follow us! Follow our voices! We will lead you out of here!"

Uncle yelled, "We have Faith; she's on her way out! Hold on to each other! Stay low to the ground—there's not much time!"

Pastor DJ and his family couldn't see anything in the thick black smoke. They had no idea whose voices they were following, but there was no time to reason, only to react. Whoever the voices in the smoke were, they had to trust them—they had to trust that Faith was okay, and they had to move quickly because the situation was dire. Faith's

bedroom, atop the garage, was engulfed in flames when they crawled by it. Anita was choking on sobs and smoke at the same time. Flames crawled up the walls of the stairway and crept along the ceiling.

"Keep following us! We're at the stairs now! Come on, keep moving! You can do it!" The wise men's voices led them with constant reassurance.

The Jones family slid, crawled, and crouched their way down the stairs, across the living room, and out the front door. All the while, they clung to each other's shirttails or pants legs so as not to get separated.

They burst onto the front lawn, into the snow. Their eyes burned and watered so badly that they could not see, and they coughed uncontrollably for several minutes. Another explosion went off in the house.

Through their coughing and the rubbing of their eyes, the family began to call, "Faith! Faith! Are you out here?"

"Here I am!" came Faith's voice from across the lawn. Her voice had never sounded so sweet. Anita ran to her and hugged her tightly; tears of joy flowed down her face. The rest of the family huddled together around Faith, crying and hugging. As they held on to each other, they heard the sound of sirens in the distance gradually getting louder.

Pastor DJ looked up and saw flames coming from every window in his house and shooting through holes in the roof. His home was totally engulfed. He searched the lawn, confused. Where were the firefighters who had helped them get out? Looking around, with the sound of sirens growing louder, he realized the firefighters hadn't arrived yet. There was no one else there.

"Faith, sweetie, who helped you get out?" Pastor DJ asked his daughter.

Faith looked up with her tear-streaked face and said, "The little wise man and his camel."

"What do you mean 'the little wise man'?" Pastor DJ asked.

Faith explained patiently. "He was an angel in disguise, but he looked like one of the little wise men in our living room. He had a camel too. I held on to the camel's tail when I was in the smoke. They brought me out here in the yard to wait for you."

"You told that little girl you were an angel?" Harold yelled in a hushed whisper from where they were hiding behind a bush.

"Well, you know, it's not exactly easy for us to explain who and what we are. Besides, she's the one who asked me if I was an angel. I just told her I am a servant of God—then she said, 'So you're like an angel in disguise?' and I said, 'Yes, but we have to leave now.'"

The next morning, the Jones family came back to their home with friends from their church. The fire department had worked all night to put out the fire, but the home was a total loss. The whole family had to be treated for smoke inhalation at the hospital.

The fire chief told them it was a miracle they had gotten out when they did because it was such a hot-burning and aggressive fire. It seemed an electric fire had started in the garage, growing out of control after the flames reached a gas can. An elderly neighbor had seen the flames and called the fire department. There was no one else around; no one stepped forward to take credit for leading them out of the fire.

It was all so unreal. The house had completely burned to the ground, and all their possessions were lost. As the family gazed upon the rubble and comforted one another, Pastor DJ tried to process the night's events. Everything had happened so fast, and that second explosion had happened so soon after they had made it to the yard. If they had spent the extra time looking for Faith instead of leaving immediately, they all would have died. He shuddered. Only the urgency and clarity of the voices in the smoke had given them confidence and reassurance that Faith was okay.

The clarity of the voices—hmm. Pastor DJ mulled it over in his head. *We could barely breathe. We were all gasping and coughing. The voices never coughed or gasped once!*

Tears welled up in his eyes as the word "angels" passed his lips. *Isn't that what Faith said last night?*

Just as Pastor DJ had that thought, he looked down. There in the mud and the snow were the wise men from their living room mantel, perfectly intact and unburned. He remembered Faith saying the angel had looked like the little wise man with the camel. Everything in the house was gone, yet here were these little decorations sitting untouched in the yard.

It must be a sign from God, he thought. He fell to his knees and burst into tears, saying, "Thank you, Lord Jesus, thank you, thank you, thank you."

Chapter Twelve

WITHOUT A HOME

The following Sunday, Pastor DJ spoke about the mysterious voices, God's divine protection, and how the Christmas statues had miraculously made it into the yard as a sign that God had been watching over his family. There were not many dry eyes in church that day. The wise men stood silent and ceramic on the edge of the pulpit as he preached.

Thunder and the wise men spent the next two years as part of the Christmas decorations at the Old Oak Baptist Church. As was usually the case, they didn't really fit with the other decorations, so they ended up on a small accent table off to the side of the fellowship hall next to an offering box. There was a lot of activity for the wise men to observe, as the fellowship hall was well used by the community. Besides Pastor DJ's karate classes, the hall played host to youth group meetings once a week, Boy Scout meetings, a women's Bible study, and a variety of other groups.

The wise men liked it there, and they would have liked to spend another Christmas at the Old Oak Baptist Church, but providence had a different plan. Prior to the Thanksgiving holiday, the church congregation participated in a food drive for local homeless shelters. They collected canned goods, dry goods, toiletry items, and other nonperishables. The Old Oak storage area was packed full of boxes containing the donations. All the boxes were loaded onto a truck and delivered for distribution to the homeless shelters. Accidentally included with all of the items was a box of Christmas decorations.

On December 12th, the three wise men and Thunder came to life once again. They found that they were on display in the front atrium of the Rescue Mission Homeless Shelter for men located in downtown Nashville. Each evening, homeless men would line up and funnel into the Rescue Mission for a hot meal and a place to sleep. Frequently some of the men were turned away because the shelter had run out of room. The wise men observed much over the next few days and started to become familiar with some of the regulars. Each night also brought new faces they hadn't seen before.

"There are certainly a lot of people who look like they could use help. I had no idea there were so many people without homes," Harold said.

"It's no wonder that the Lord has brought us here," Uncle agreed. "I am sure there will be some good we can do this Christmas."

"Look, here comes Charlie again. He talks to us every time he sees us. Do you think he actually knows something about us?" Chip said.

"He talks incessantly," Harold answered. "I personally don't think all of the clockwork in his head is keeping the right time."

Charlie stepped out of the food line and walked right up to the table where the wise men were displayed. He smiled, prominently showing the spaces that had once displayed two of his front teeth. His skin was as dark as Harold's was, but he had a spackling of gray in his matted afro and scraggly beard.

"Well, hello fellas! It's so good to see you! Ol' Charlie just wanted to stop by, say hi, and tell you a little about my day. Oh lordy, it was a cold one out there today. I thank the Lord that I have this here shelter wheres I kin stay warm tonight."

"Hello, Charlie! Can you hear me? My name is Chip!" Chip shouted. Charlie smiled and kept rambling on about his day.

"…and then this nice lady handed me a sack with half a sandwich and apple inside it—oh, I tells you, the Lord does provide. You just have to have faith and trust in him…"

"We do believe—we do trust! We are servants of God!" Chip was still yelling, trying to see if Charlie could hear him or not.

"You're just wasting your time, Chip. You can clearly see that this man is…well, he just isn't *well*. He rambles on like this every time he sees us. I think I saw him talking to the tree in the corner last night too," Harold said.

Charlie kept on talking. He got his share of stares and judgmental looks from the other men who were slowly passing by, but none of that seemed to affect him. Nothing seemed to affect his positive out-look on life, either. Charlie seemed content and happy, even though he looked like he had been living on the streets for years. He wore tattered clothes and carried an old drab-green knapsack, which contained all of his worldly possessions. When he talked, he never complained about his situation. He always had something positive to say about his day and how the Lord had taken care of him.

On this day, one of the mission employees noticed Charlie talking to the ceramic statues. He smiled and walked over to the elderly black man.

"Hey, Charlie, you better get back in line and go get your plate of food," the man said, placing his hand on Charlie's shoulder.

Charlie turned his head and smiled at the man.

"Yes sir, Mr. Caleb, I's sure am glad to come here and eat this here wonderful food that you provide. I sure don't want to miss out on that." Charlie closed his eyes for a moment and breathed in deeply through his nostrils. "Um-um, its sure does smell good, Mr. Caleb, yes sir," Charlie said as he exhaled. "I was just talkin' to my little friends here."

Caleb smiled and said, "Yes, I see that. Why don't you tell your friends good-bye, and let's go get you a plate, Mr. Charlie."

"Good-bye, my three little friends. I's talk to you later," Charlie said as he turned to walk with Caleb.

"Gruuumph," came a grunt from Thunder.

Charlie stopped and cocked his head back over his shoulder.

"I'm sorry; I didn't mean to leave you out, little camel! I's talk to you later too."

"Did you hear that!" said Chip. "He *can* hear us. He heard Thunder. Did you see that, Harold?"

Harold pondered. "Hmm, I do have to admit that was an awfully strange coincidence—if it *was* a coincidence."

Meanwhile, a few blocks away, a bus was pulling into the downtown bus depot from Memphis, Tennessee, about a three-and-a-half-hour drive away. A hodgepodge of people filtered off the Greyhound and collected their bags and luggage. One of the people was JW.

JW stepped off the final step of the bus with his head held high and his eyes alert. He flowed along with the line of people for a moment, then stepped to the side to let those behind him pass by. He took a deep breath and drank in his surroundings. To most, this was just another stop, nothing spectacular, certainly not on the list of sights to see in Nashville. To JW, however, even the plainness of the depot held a special emotional connection; just seeing the large sign over the door that read *Welcome to Nashville* made his heart beat a little faster.

"It's been a long time," JW whispered to himself.

JW had been to London, Uganda, and several other locations. This was the first time he had been back to the United States in almost two years. His flight had landed in New York City a day earlier. A flight to Memphis was available a full eight hours before he could fly into Nashville, so he decided to take it and catch a bus the rest of the way home.

Home? JW wondered if he really had a home anymore. All of his traveling had taken a toll on his finances. He'd had to work some odd jobs in Europe in order to buy a ticket back to the U.S. The bus ticket from Memphis to Nashville had him down to his last few dollars. JW just had two pieces of luggage: a backpack and a medium-sized duffel bag. He had learned to travel light over the past two years, and the weight on his heart wasn't nearly as heavy as it once had been, either.

"JW!" called a voice at the bus terminal. A young man around JW's age came walking across the terminal.

JW turned around. "Hey, Mike! Thanks so much for helping me out, man. It's good to see you."

Mike was thin and lanky, with shoulder-length brown hair. He was wearing a denim jacket and blue jeans with a tattered hole in one knee and a black concert T-shirt from some local band.

JW reached out to meet Mike with a handshake.

Mike shook his hand. "Long time no see."

Mike was an acquaintance JW had met in college the semester before he left. He had once told JW that if he needed a place to crash when he got back into town, just call—so JW had decided to take him up on his offer. He just needed a place to stay for a few days while he figured out his living situation and looked for a job.

JW had considered calling the Jones family, but he was nervous about it. He had promised to keep in touch, but for the past two years, he hadn't so much as called or sent a postcard. He'd had every good intention of staying in touch with them and didn't really have an excuse as to why he hadn't—unless it was because he'd needed so badly to just leave everything behind for a while. Anyway, now he felt guilty about calling them right away, especially since he was almost out of money. He knew the Joneses would offer to help him in any way they could, but that would just make him feel even more guilty. He thought it would be best to stop by and surprise them after he got settled somewhere.

Somehow it was easier to call Mike, whom he didn't know very well, than to call the people who had been like a second family to him.

"Do you still play the guitar?" Mike asked as JW picked up his bags and they walked toward the parking lot.

"Every once in a while," JW answered. "I haven't really played much lately."

"I stopped going to school about the same time you did. I pretty much play in the band full-time now." Mike added enthusiastically, "We recognized a record-company scout in the audience at our last gig—maybe we're getting close to hitting it big!"

Back at the homeless shelter, things were winding down for the night. Dinner and cleanup were done. People were filtering in and out of the showers, and others were settling into their bunks.

Harold, Chip, and Uncle could hear a man's angry voice arguing with Caleb down the hall. "What do you mean, you're full? Where am I supposed to sleep tonight? Isn't this supposed to be a shelter?" he yelled.

Caleb's firm but calm voice replied, "Let me call one of the other shelters for you, sir, and see if they have any beds available."

"I've been to those other places, and I don't want to go back! I want to come here!"

Next, they heard Charlie's pleasant, friendly voice, "Now, now, you need to lower your voice. There be folks trying to go to sleep here, and I knows you wouldn't want to disturb no one. Mr. Caleb here is just a-doing his job—it ain't his fault all the beds is full."

"Crazy Charlie, you stay out of this! I don't need no mentally ill, ravin' lunatic to tell me to lower my voice!"

Caleb cut him off politely but loudly. "Sir! Sir, I've explained the situation to you—now, you need to leave the property, or I will be forced to call the police. Do you understand?"

The angry voice calmed down a bit, but its tone was just as bitter as when it had been yelling. "Fine, fine, I'm leaving. I didn't want to stay at this stupid religious freak show anyway."

Not far away, JW got out of Mike's pickup truck and followed him up the concrete steps to a small, rundown, two-bedroom apartment in downtown Nashville. "We don't have a lot of room, but you'll be fine on the couch for a couple of days," Mike said as he unlocked the door.

"I've been thinking," Harold said in the quiet that had finally settled over the shelter. "I was thinking about our purpose during those Christmases that we spent at Mr. and Mrs. Miller's house. Do you remember that we even discussed whether God might have sent us there to retire?"

"But then we had the times at the nursing home and with the Jones family," added Uncle thoughtfully. "So retirement wasn't it after all."

"If we hadn't been there during the fire, who knows what would have happened?" said Chip. "So why *do* you think we spent those Christmases at the Millers' house?"

"Well, Chip, that's where my thoughts started." Harold said, and then he was quiet for a moment before he went on. "But as I pondered, it came to me that those days were just a season in our existence. Then I mulled it over and thought, what *have* been the seasons of our existence? This is what I have come up with:

"Our first memories are of the factory, where we were made by human hands. Then something happened; the Lord gave us a spirit of life and of knowing. These things were the season of our creation. Then we passed through the fire and awoke at the store in London. This was our birth. At Clemons's Store, we were lost and knew no purpose in life. I, like a fool, thought our existence was meaningless, or perhaps some strange kind of punishment. This was similar to the human state of living without God. Then the angel came to us and revealed our purpose. This was the season of our deliverance from ignorance and our revelation of truth."

"Go on," Chip said, with a hint of wonderment in his voice. Harold continued, "The time we spent at the orphanage was like the season of our childhood. We were full of innocence and had faith like children. Then, through Jason's eyes, we came to know suffering and pain, loneliness and disappointment. In that one night, we grew much. We came to realize that some questions don't have answers and that happiness is a choice, not a given. This was a season of our coming into maturity." Harold paused for a moment.

"So what season was the time we spent with the Millers?" asked Chip again.

"That is where my pondering got stuck. It is obvious to me that our conversations with Jason brought about a transformation in the way we think and talk. We brought with us our childlike faith, but we were confronted with a situation that we did not have easy answers for. We were able to create a bond with Jason by talking about the children of the orphanage and comparing them to his experiences in foster care. Before the night was over, Jason realized that his real pain was not from the injuries to his body, but from the scars and injuries to his heart and soul."

"I agree with your thoughts, Harold," said Uncle. "If I may add to what you are saying, I think our time with the Millers was a time of growth too—the type of growth that takes time and reflection. We saw a devoted and happy husband and wife grow old together. We learned about many of the evils of the outside world through Mr. Miller's TV news shows. We learned that the lives of humans are full of pain, disappointment, and death. Yes, I believe we have changed, and like adult humans, we have lost some of our innocence. It has even crossed my thoughts to wonder how many Christmases we have left. Will the life God has given us be taken away some day? I would say this has been the season of our continued maturity—our night with Jason was just the beginning of that season. Suffering and death were new and troubling to us then, but now I can say with assurance that whether in life or in death, we belong to God. The same is true of the humans we have learned to care about."

Chip listened intently to Harold and Uncle and pondered every word. "Do you suppose that all of these things—all of these seasons—have been preparing us for something yet to come?" proposed Chip.

"Perhaps my friend, perhaps," Harold said solemnly.

Suddenly, the wise men became aware that a man was moving quickly from the exterior door into the atrium. He lurched into the dim lighting, and they got a good glimpse of him before his features were lost in shadow again. The man was unshaven and wearing a tattered overcoat with an old brown scarf doubled around his neck just underneath his greasy brown hair. He walked straight into the middle of the atrium, looked to the left and then to the right, and then he walked toward the wise men mumbling to himself under his breath.

"I'll show them!" he sputtered. The wise men realized it was the same angry voice they had heard talking to Caleb earlier.

The man grabbed the wise men and shoved the ceramic statues into his overcoat, clutching them with his left arm so they could not fall out the bottom. He darted out the door into the cold night.

Chapter Thirteen

INTO THE LION'S DEN

The three wise men and Thunder spent the night under a bridge with the angry man. The night was filled with the unfamiliar noises of traffic, trash blowing in the wind, sirens, and even screams in the distance. The man slept close by them, curled in a tight ball. He tossed, turned, mumbled, and snored all night.

"I don't like this at all," Harold stated. "We have been stolen. There is no telling what this man might do with us."

"No, no! Give me that! Give it to me!" the man burst out.

"He even talks angry in his sleep," Chip noted.

The next morning the man stuffed them back inside his coat and walked for several blocks. The wise men could hear the noises of the city: cars, buses, and the footfalls of people bustling down the sidewalks. Then they heard a door open, and the noise of the street went quiet. The man pulled the three ceramic figures out of his coat and set them on a countertop next to a cash register. The counter on both sides was cluttered with books and papers.

The man behind the counter was sitting on a chrome swivel-top barstool at a tall worktable. His back was to the cash register, and he was casually thumbing through a book.

"How much can I get for these?" the man said impatiently.

"What did you steal this time, Lucas?" The storeowner didn't even look up.

"I brought you something good this time, Hector…um…Mr. Boa, sir. These here are some fancy art statues like those ones you got in the window."

This comment caused the storeowner to swivel around slowly in his chair with one eyebrow raised in suspicion but a little interest, too.

Hector Boa was a big man both in height and in weight. He stood about six foot four and was about forty pounds overweight. His skin was pasty white, as if he had never had a tan in all of his life. The blackness of his hair, which was drawn back tight against his head into a short ponytail, made his skin look whiter that it actually was. His face had several points of interest. Chief among them was the widow's peak on his forehead, which pointed downward to his nose. His eyebrows, in turn, pointed back up at his hairline. Black as the rest of his hair, each eyebrow had some extra-long hairs right in the middle that curved up to give the illusion of points at the tops of his eyebrows.

"Well, let's see what you got here." Hector picked up the ceramic pieces and looked them over.

The thief watched impatiently. Hector's meticulously trimmed goatee had thin lines that curved to points at the side of his mouth and down to the point of his chin. Between his chin and lower lip was one small dot of hair marooned like a solitary island surrounded by shaven skin. His short sideburns also narrowed to a point, which flowed into a thin line of hair down his jawline and along the top half of his slight double chin.

The other points of interest on his face included the small, matching sterling-silver hoop rings in his left eyebrow, left nostril, and left lower lip. He had larger hoop earrings on the lobe of each ear, and three blood-red faux ruby studs going up the side of each ear.

The fact that Mr. Boa wore a black T-shirt, black leather vest, black jeans, and black motorcycle boots confirmed the fact that he was trying to convey a dark, mysterious, and slightly creepy impression to those who ventured into his store. He enjoyed the feeling he got when he perceived that people were unnerved by his size and appearance.

Not that it worked on everyone. Lucas wasn't actually all that unnerved by Hector Boa, but he had learned from past experience that if he played to Hector's ego, he usually got a better price for the items he fenced at the Lion's Den Pawn Shop.

"I don't know if I can resell this junk," Hector said with a disinterested look on his face.

"No, sir, these are some nice pieces of art. Um, the person that had 'em didn't know what he had. I got them for a real steal." Lucas had a hard time concealing his grin as he talked.

"A real steal indeed," huffed Harold.

"He stole us all right," added Chip, followed by an agreeing "Grumpf" from Thunder.

"Well, if we have learned anything in our short existence, it is that no matter the circumstances, God has a plan for us. Either it is part of

God's plan that we ended up here, or God will take what was meant for evil and make it into something good," said Uncle.

Lucas and Hector haggled as the wise men discussed their situation and reported what each could see of the store from his perspective.

The Lion's Den was a cluttered mess by most standards. However, it was loosely categorized into different sections. The store itself was long and narrow with an open doorway at the far end, directly opposite the door at the front where customers entered. A tool section in the front right corner of the store displayed all manner of hand tools: electric saws, cordless and corded drills, grinders, sanders, and an assortment of plastic toolboxes.

Next to the tools and opposite the cash register, all shapes and sizes of musical instruments hung on a wall between a large stock of battered guitars. On the floor in front of the music wall sat a long line of used cowboy boots of all sizes and colors. Above the musical instruments, stretching all the way up to the twelve-foot ceiling, were hundreds of randomly placed pegs, nails, and screws. Hanging there was a large assortment of cowboy hats, spurs, bridles, leather goods, and many items that were hard to identify.

Over the door, a mounted lion's head glared down from above a painted sign that read *The Lion's Den.* On each side of the four-foot-wide doorway were other heads of once-living creatures. Each creature had fangs bared in a permanent snarl, with a full-size crocodile skin on the left side of the hall and a full-size alligator skin on the right. The long hallway at the back of the store opened into several small rooms with windows on each side. These rooms displayed what Hector considered his prized artifacts: skins and head mounts of exotic animals and a collection of shields, spears, swords, and ancient-looking statues depicting various eastern religions. Crowning the collection was Hector's favorite room, containing voodoo artifacts and items of supposed magical significance and power.

After some haggling, Hector paid Lucas eight dollars for the set of wise men and placed them on display in the front window. "Maybe some sentimental fool will buy these for a Christmas present," Hector said as he walked back and took his seat once again at his worktable. Above the worktable, Hector's personal collection of books lined a shelf: *Ceremonial Magic*, *The Complete Book of Spells*, *Guide to the Black Arts*, *Witchcraft*, and *Voodoo*. Hector pulled a book off the shelf and started reading.

"What is that?" Uncle asked in a hushed tone.

Out the window, the threesome saw a strange form moving back and forth through the street. It circled and weaved back and forth around people who were standing and walking, but the people did not seem to notice it. It was a dark mist in the shape of a man-like creature without legs.. It snaked through the air effortlessly, appearing to examine the people it circled.

As the creature came closer, the wise men could make out the features of a face—or so they thought. When it began to circle and examine the people on the sidewalk just outside the store, they could see the face even more clearly, and they all watched in fear. The face was changing, continually morphing from one face to another, each with its own unique features. At times, it seemed as if two faces were trying to appear at once, and their slight misalignment would give the face a fuzzy, distorted look. The body whisked around like smoke blown by an invisible, swirling wind.

Lucas was gone. Behind the wise men, Hector was lighting a stick of incense and mumbling to himself. The dark form switched direction and came into the store, passing effortlessly through the window to hover right above the wise men. The wise men said nothing, but they suddenly realized that they could hear voices—dark, haunting voices.

"Yes, yes, he is coming along very nicely…his fascination has taken root…he seeks knowledge of all things but rejects Truth…yes, yes, we speak what our eyes have seen…detestable, detestable human, deserving of his fate…yes, yes, you speak what is right…his destruction is certain; his judgment must be sealed…" The voices hissed and echoed and gargled the words in frightful harmony.

As Hector's voice rose in intensity, cruel, callous laughter arose from the thing hovering in the window. "He beckons and commands us to come and do his bidding." More malicious laughter rang out. "Oh, he invites us in, Captain, he evokes that of which he knows no understanding. Shall we give him a sign? Shall we feed his desire for power, O Captain and Commander of us all?" The voices rose in frenzy and started overlapping, cutting each other off like the sound of coyotes yapping on a cold, still night.

Then a voice cut them all off: "Silence!"

The commanding voice continued, and the wise men stayed frozen in silence, listening with growing fear. "We must let him choose. We must let him set his own snare. His heart has already turned, for it is out of the human heart that evil thoughts, murder, adultery, sexual immorality, theft, false testimony, and slander come. Let his fascination be his downfall! Let his desire grow for those black arts he thinks he understands. He is a fool. Let us go to him—let us move closer so

150

he can feel our presence in his bones. We need not give him a sign. We need only to feed his desire for the unknown malevolence he imagines he can control."

"Yes, yes, good, good, you speak what is right, O Captain and Commander!" came the chorus of voices. The thing then moved farther into the store where the wise men could only hear the hissed whispers of their conversations.

The wise men somehow feared that the thing they had just seen would most certainly hear them if they spoke. It was the first time any of them had actually experienced true fear and dread. After a few minutes, the store became quiet again, and the thing swooshed by them through the window and out of their sight. They still said nothing.

About a minute later, a young man came running across the street toward the store.

"Look!" Chip announced. It was JW. He trotted across the street behind a passing car, hopped up on the sidewalk, and walked into the Lion's Den Pawn Shop. But the wise men stilled their cheers of recognition, for at the same time that JW entered, the wise men saw the dark mass come around the corner and into the store again.

JW paused under the lion's head, then, seeing Hector sitting at his worktable, said, "Excuse me, sir. I was wondering if you might be hiring. I'm willing to work full-time or part-time if you have anything available."

Immediately, the creature slowed, moving side to side in the air like a cobra mesmerized by the sound of a snake charmer's flute. The gravelly, hissing voice of the Commander spoke. "What is the voice I hear? Where has it traveled from and into mine ears?"

"We do not know from where it comes, our captain…we are one with you…we heard it too, but do not know from where it comes," came the chorus of voices.

The dark mass snaked around the store and swam through the air, looking at the objects and artifacts in the store. It circled and hovered, coming closer to the wise men, and then it moved down and came face to face with them. It paused there, moving back and forth as if studying them.

"What is this I feel?" came the Captain's voice. "What manner of us are you? Come out of those objects; show yourselves." The wise men remained still and silent. The Captain paused as if unsure of himself. "What is this presence I feel?"

"We know not…we know not…feel it we do, Captain, but we know not where it is or where it comes from."

"Say this thing…say this thing which we heard. Say it for me again," said the Captain.

"Look, look, look, look, look! Look! Look!" The many voices repeated the word that Chip had spoken. Each time, the tone and fluctuation changed and came together until it merged into one solid voice that was an exact reproduction of Chip's: "Look! Look! Look…look!"

The mass of creatures was moving around the room again, almost in a pacing motion. "Yes, yes," hissed the Captain's voice. "This is the voice I did hear…I know all voices of us from all time and time before time…I know every voice of us fallen and every voice of us who are still true…I know every voice and the name of every voice."

"Yes, yes, it is true, Captain, it is true."

"But I do not know this voice or who it comes from!"

"How can it be, Captain? How can it be? We do not know."

After a long pause followed by more pacing, the Captain spoke again. "Let not the voice trouble us any longer. We must travel…we have distances to cover…we must attend to other business now. Let us leave this place and this mystery behind us."

"Yes, yes, Captain. Let us go now."

The dark mass swept out into the street and snaked its way along the sidewalk until it was out of sight. The wise men still didn't dare make a sound or speak a word.

While all of this was happening, JW received an answer from Hector. "Did you see a 'help wanted' sign in the window, boy?" Hector said as he swiveled in his chair to give JW an intimidating, expressionless stare down.

Taken aback by the man's curt response, JW tried to stammer an answer.

Hector perceived that his intended intimidation had worked, and he broke into a big smile and softened his tone. "Well, son, as you can see, I don't have a sign in the window, so that means I am not hiring. But please, come in! Look around. You might find something you'll want to come back for when you do find a job." Hector broke into guffaws of laughter.

JW wasn't sure why the man was laughing, but his curt attitude had flipped so quickly to teasing that JW wasn't sure if the guy was just messing with him or if he was perhaps a little eccentric.

"Ah, okay…thanks, sorry to bother you. Maybe I'll just look around a little while I'm here." JW faked an interest in the guitars, which was better than continuing his conversation with the man, who was starting to give him the creeps. He browsed toward the door, intent on leaving, when he stopped suddenly in front of the display window. Thunder caught his eye first, and then he realized they were all there. He started to move toward the figurines, but Hector had stood and was watching him.

JW shot one last glance back toward the owner, then exited the store. He paused outside and peered in the window at the three wise men. "I remember you guys so well. You seemed so real to me," he said aloud. Then he turned and headed down the street.

Unbeknownst to JW, the dark mass of creatures passed right by him as he turned the corner.

Chapter Fourteen

BREAK OUT

JW had put in twenty-three job applications in the past week, but still had no luck in finding a job. He tried to stay busy during the day and hung out in the evenings at Mike's apartment. JW was thankful that Mike and his roommate, Matt, were allowing him to crash on their couch, but he didn't want to overstay his welcome, so he tried to stay out of their way. Besides, he didn't exactly fit in with Mike and Matt's lifestyle; they spent a lot of time going to parties and dance clubs. On the plus side, Mike and Matt played in a band, so some nights JW had the place to himself. He liked the peace and quiet. The only thing bad about hanging out in the apartment by himself was that it gave him too much time to think, and that's where JW found himself the evening of December 23rd—sitting alone in the apartment, thinking.

He hadn't thought getting a job would be this hard, and he couldn't start looking for his own place without some income. He was still upset that the life-insurance money had gone so fast. Had he been irresponsible to do so much traveling? Should he have stayed in the States and gone back to school? He doubted so many of his decisions. But the traveling had taught him a lot about himself—he had grown and matured, hadn't he? His travels had helped him escape the pain of his parents' death to some degree, but now, with no money to travel on a whim to the next spot, his emotions were beginning to catch up with him. Being back in Nashville in familiar surroundings brought back memories and feelings that weighed heavily on him.

Even something as simple as seeing a particular restaurant on a particular corner brought tears to his eyes when he remembered eating there with his mom and dad one bright sunny afternoon. *So silly!* JW thought, *to get all choked up just from looking at a stupid restaurant.*

Whether he wanted to admit it or not, that was one reason he was at Mike's apartment in the downtown area. It was why he hoped to find an apartment of his own in the same area—fewer memories there. He had grown up in the suburbs, so this part of the city held far less pain for him to deal with. That was the reason he still hadn't brought himself to call his best friend, Isaiah, or even let the Jones family know he was back in town. When his parents died, JW had been forced to let go of more than he thought he could bear. He had questioned everything he had ever believed. He still hadn't processed all of his thoughts and feelings. He missed his mom and dad so much.

As he sat there on the couch, he thought about watching TV, but he wasn't motivated enough to get up and turn it on. JW's mind drifted back to some of his first memories of his mother. He remembered when he was five years old at the orphanage and how desperate he was to have a family. He laughed at himself every time he remembered the three wise men and that funny little camel, Thunder…what a silly name for a camel. He remembered falling asleep on the front pew of the sanctuary and dreaming that the little men and the camel had come to life and promised to help him find a family. It was such a vivid dream; sometimes he had wondered if it had really happened. But it had to have been a dream; even their names were things only a five-year-old child would come up with—Uncle, Chip, and Harold…as in "Hark, the Herald Angels Sing." He remembered telling his mom about them and how he had been so convinced that they were real. Elizabeth had told him that maybe the dream meant something; maybe God had given him the dream so that he wouldn't lose hope.

JW had wrapped his arms around Elizabeth's neck and excitedly said, "You mean you think God is telling me I am going to get a family?" Elizabeth had hesitated, fearful that maybe she had said the wrong thing, afraid that she might be setting him up for disappointment.

JW still remembered the look on his mother's face that early morning after she carried him back to the boys' dorm room. He remembered the warmth of her smile and the concern in her eyes. He remembered saying, "I hope the mom God gives me is just like you." He remembered that she had not said anything in return, but had just given him a big hug so that he wouldn't see the tears welling up in her eyes.

But of course he had seen them.

When he was older, she told him, "That was the moment. That was the moment I knew I was going to adopt you."

She explained that, as she had searched for an encouraging explanation for JW's dream, a thought had washed over her: *Why don't you be his mother?* It was a thought filled with peace and contentment, as if it came from God himself. She told JW that over the years she had come to accept that his dream had been meant for her, that God had spoken to her heart in that moment, and that was when she knew she was going to be his mother.

Tears rolled down JW's cheeks as he let his thoughts drift. He remembered Elizabeth coming back to the orphanage with a man about her age. It was several days after Christmas. JW saw them come in, then go into an office and shut the door. They spent a long time in the office talking to Father Andrew and some of the other orphanage staff. JW was watching some older boys play a board game when he looked up and saw Elizabeth crossing the room with Father Andrew and the man.

"JW, may we have a word with you please?" asked Father Andrew.

JW wondered if he was in some kind of trouble as he followed them to a quiet corner of the room.

Elizabeth was acting a little strange, and JW wondered what was going on. She knelt and put her arm around his shoulders and said, "JW, I would like you to meet a friend of mine. This is Hiram Adams. He lives across the ocean in the United States."

"Nice to meet you, JW." Hiram shook JW's hand as if he was a grownup. JW liked his warm and sincere smile.

Elizabeth looked back and forth from Hiram to Father Andrew with a big, strange smile on her face. She laughed nervously and bent her head to JW's eye level. JW could see tears forming in her eyes and prepared himself for some sort of bad news.

Elizabeth cleared her throat. "JW, you know the other day when you told me that all you wanted for Christmas was a family?"

"Uh-huh." JW had nodded.

"Well, I'm sorry you didn't get one on Christmas Day, but, well, what I am trying to say is, how would you like to be part of our family?"

JW was shocked and confused. "You mean you want me to come and live with you and your mom and dad?"

Everyone laughed, but JW knew they were just laughing because he had misunderstood something.

"What I am asking you, JW, is, how would you like to have *me* be your mom, and Hiram here will be your dad?"

"Really?" JW froze. He wondered if he was dreaming—it didn't seem real.

"Yes, really," Hiram said, bending down to one knee next to Elizabeth. "We want to make sure it's okay with you, though. You don't have to answer now—I'm willing to come and visit you some more so you can get to know me a little better."

"Yes! It's okay with me!" There was a long pause as JW looked from Elizabeth, Hiram, Father Andrew, then back to Elizabeth again. "I got a family! A real family for Christmas!" They all embraced as Father Andrew looked on, smiling.

JW still had to spend a couple more weeks at the orphanage, but his mom and dad came every day to spend time with him. He liked Hiram as much as he liked Elizabeth. Of course, they had to get married before they could adopt him. The whole situation was a little strange for both sides of the family—it all seemed so rushed. Hiram's family wondered what in the world had gotten into him. What would cause him to fly off to Europe, get married, and adopt a child all at the same time? Boy, how the rumors flew back home in the States!

Elizabeth's parents weren't any less worried about their daughter—it was all so out of character for her. She was a planner and a worrier; she was never spontaneous! Why was she rushing into marriage with no planning and no big ceremony? What on earth did she think she was doing adopting a five-year-old boy? Had she gone mad?

Even people at the orphanage had their questions, but Father Andrew was their biggest supporter. He convinced the adoption board that the adoption was in JW's best interest; it was nothing less than an answer to prayer. Father Andrew was so bold that he told the board, "If anyone on this board questions the appropriateness of this adoption, then they are also questioning my faith in God!" No one dared question *that*, so the adoption was approved unanimously.

JW had heard the story told and retold as he grew up. His mom and dad laughed at all the comments, cautions, and questions they'd had to deal with from their families. But they had no regrets. They both spoke of knowing how everything they had done was part of God's plan, no matter how crazy it seemed to everyone else. They didn't care how things might have looked, or the motives people attributed to their actions. They believed in their hearts that they were doing the right thing, and their strong and loving marriage proved them right, year after year.

Why, God, why did you let them die? The thought snapped JW out of his trance. He reached up and wiped the tears off his cheeks with his sleeve. He looked at the clock: it was 9:45 p.m. He had been sitting on the couch doing nothing but thinking for the past two hours.

Where were the other guys? *I don't remember Mike and Matt saying anything about a gig tonight,* JW thought to himself. Just then, Mike's truck and two other cars pulled up in front of the apartment. Mike, Matt, and a mix of eight guys and girls exited the vehicles with loud talking and laughter. They funneled their way up the steps and into the apartment. JW sighed. *So much for going to bed early.*

"Hey, JW!" Mike called out as he came through the door. "A few of our friends from the night club where we play are coming to hang with us for a while."

The group burst through the door and settled into the cramped apartment. Most of them smelled of cigarette smoke and alcohol.

A couple of hours passed. JW tried to politely stay out of the way and occasionally socialize with the loud and boisterous group. But after a couple hours of small talk and listening to people complain about their life's tragedies, such as getting traffic tickets and warnings from landlords about playing their music too loudly, JW was feeling the need to take a walk and get some fresh air.

JW drank the last bit of his Pepsi, stood up, and set the plastic cup on the counter next to the sink. "I'm going to walk down to the twenty-four-hour grocery and pick up a couple of things," he announced as he grabbed his coat.

"Okay, dude, see ya later!" someone said as JW walked out the door. A couple of people rolled their eyes behind JW's back as if to say, *Don't hurry back, you party pooper.* As JW walked out the door, a girl leaned to the guy sitting next to her and asked, "What did you put in that guy's Pepsi?"

"Oh, just a little something to help him loosen up—he didn't look like he was havin' a very good time. I just thought I'd help him out a little, y'know?"

JW had walked a couple of blocks when he started feeling dizzy. He shook his head and kept moving. He cut across a small wooded city park to save time in getting to the grocery store. As he walked, he noticed a couple of homeless men with army-green sleeping bags huddled together between a tree and a picnic table. Maybe he should have stayed on the sidewalk instead of taking the shortcut across the park. The dizziness came back. He blinked hard a couple of times and shook it off again. *Man, what's wrong with me? Maybe I'm just getting tired.*

As he came to the sidewalk on the other side of the park, he looked up the street and remembered that this was where he had seen the wise man and camel the other day. JW looked both ways and trotted across the street and up half a block to the Lion's Den Pawn Shop. He came up to the bar-covered window and looked in. Sure enough, they were still there.

"I wish I could get a better look at you guys." He cupped his hands to his face to block some of the glare from the streetlights. This set of wise men looked just like the one in his memories. Looking at the little faces was like seeing old friends. Their brightly painted features were so expertly done; they did look as though they could talk.

The early memories of the orphanage came back to him again. He remembered how lonely he had been as a child. He felt the same loneliness now. He had such joyful memories of his mom and dad, and all of that joy had started at the orphanage, but that joy was gone now.

JW smiled as the memories flipped through his mind like a book being thumbed by an invisible hand. But the invisible hand always seemed to flip through the pages too quickly, and once again he was seeing the tragedy at the end of his book. The joy of remembering his parents mixed with the pain of their loss caused tears to well up in his eyes as he peered through the window.

"Why did you let them die God…why?" JW sniffed. The striped shadows that fell across the wise men seemed like bars blocking him from the life he wanted. His sorrow and pain turned to anger and self-pity.

"All I ever wanted was a family. All those years I believed you answered my prayers. I believed in miracles. But why would you give me a family only to take it all away from me again?"

In all of the traveling he had done, JW wasn't sure if he had been searching for something or merely running away. He had found comfort in traveling to London, and hope and inspiration when he traveled to Uganda. In Singapore, Manila, and Shanghai he had left more and more of the past behind. He'd thought that he had found some healing. He had seen so much and learned about the sufferings and joys of other people in the world. When he was traveling from place to place, life seemed to make sense somehow. But none of that mattered right now, standing on a cold, dark sidewalk in Nashville. The memories flashed to an end. The emotions attached to them also came full circle. The joy warmed his heart, but the anger burned in his mind. Anger was quickly replaced by the sunken coldness of sorrow, and finally, hope faded into something like an unreachable dream.

JW bumped his head gently against one of the bars covering the glass and felt woozy all of a sudden. He realized he had been talking aloud. He looked around, self-conscious, wondering if anyone had seen him. That strange, spacey feeling came back, and he couldn't shake it off this time. "Man! What's wrong with me? I am feeling really strange!"

It was then that JW also noticed a strange coldness. His coat was sufficient for the cold of the night, but this was a different cold: an eerie cold that seemed to be hovering nearby. He shook his head and rubbed his eyes. He had the strange feeling that someone was watching him, and he didn't feel safe. JW moved quickly away from the window. He headed briskly down the sidewalk in the opposite direction from the grocery store. He was not sure where he was going. He just knew he had to get away from this place.

When JW had first approached the window, the wise men were discussing what their mission could possibly be, so they were excited to see JW come up to the glass and peer in.

Several days had passed since they had seen the strange creature. On that day, they had remained silent until they were sure it was gone. Over the past few days, they had discussed much about their situation. They reasoned that the creature, or *creatures,* they had seen must be demons—the fallen angels they had heard stories about, and that the angel of the Lord had warned them of when they were at Clemons's Store. It was obvious that the demons had somehow sensed their presence, and certainly, they had heard Chip's voice. That unnerved them the most. Just one word spoken by Chip, and the demons had known it was not human. They had talked of knowing "all the voices of us," which the wise men interpreted as the voices of the spiritual world—the voices of the angels and the voices of the fallen ones. Harold surmised that angels must be highly intelligent and eons old. If that was so, then they had certainly lived long enough to know all manner of things, including all the voices of the spiritual realm.

It was 11:53 p.m.

"I think something is wrong with JW. He looks upset," observed Harold.

"Won't he be excited to see us come to life again when it turns midnight? Then we can see what he needs and maybe help him," said Chip excitedly.

Uncle spoke up. "Do you think it is wise for us to be so bold in letting him see us when we come to life? After all, it has been many years… he was just a child last time. We've always avoided letting people see us."

Just then, sinister laughter and hissing voices came from the store behind the wise men.

"So we were correct; we did feel a presence in these little statues…and what is this that my ears do hear but three voices!" came the Commander's voice, followed by the collective sound of other voices: "Yes, yes—three voices, O Captain of us."

The mass of creatures swirled in front of the wise men and snaked back and forth before their eyes.

The Captain spoke again. "We have been watching for you…we have been listening to you. Come to life, you say? What do you mean when you say 'come to life'? We are anxious to see this." His voice was calm and almost sounded friendly.

The wise men said nothing.

"Do not treat me as a fool with your silence! Speak to us!" The Captain's voice yelled, ending with a gravelly hiss that would be fitting for a dragon.

"We are servants of the Lord Jesus Christ, and we have nothing to say to you," said Harold confidently.

"Oh, we beg your forgiveness, mighty servants of the Most High King of Kings and Lord of Lords," said the Captain.

"Forgive us! Forgive us! Servants of the Most High!" echoed the choir of other voices.

"I am The Commander, The Captain of the many of us. We are many, but we are one. By what names may we call you, O servants of the Most High?" The demon's voice sounded reverent and sincere when he talked, but Uncle and Harold instinctively knew that they were being mocked.

Chip, being more innocent, said, "My name is Chip."

Uncle immediately cut him off. "We have nothing to say."

"Come, come now, you must be the one referred to as Uncle, and the other is Harold...we have been listening to you for longer than you know." The Commander laughed. His voice had started off nice, but it trailed off into a sinister tone by the end of the sentence.

"What it is that you want with us?" asked Harold.

The mass of demons started weaving back and forth and swirling again. Calm and confident, the Commander's voice became nonchalant and cold. "Oh dear, little servants of God—though you are peculiar... and have caused us a passing curiosity...we desire nothing of you. For you have already delivered into our hands something we all find much more interesting—this one you so affectionately call JW."

The commander used the word *JW* like punctuation at the end of his sentence. As soon as it was typed onto the page of the wise men's minds, the mass of demons turned and passed through the glass. They began to circle around JW like the dark shadows of sharks in deep water.

The wise men stood frozen in their ceramic state, horrified. They could not hear the demons on the other side of the glass, but they could see them circling. JW looked confused and tormented. He brought his hands up to his eyes, rubbed them, and shook his head as if trying to shake off a bad thought or feeling. JW turned his tear-streaked, anguished face to the window once more, then turned and quickly moved in the direction he had come. The demons followed him like a wisp of smoke following a torch.

"I can move my arms!" yelled Uncle.

"Me too!" shouted the other two.

Never had they wanted their midnight transformation to happen more quickly! The fear and dread the demons had put into their hearts quickly turned into a kind of protective parental anger, and all they could think about was protecting JW in any way they possibly could.

"Grumph!" Off galloped Thunder. He always seemed to be the first one to gain complete freedom of movement, and he wasted no time moving into action.

Thunder moved across the display window and stopped midway on the window ledge. He narrowed his eyes with focus and determination. With a quick snort from his nostrils, he took off again at full speed. He deliberately ran smack into a tall, skinny Hindu statue with four arms that was standing on one foot. It leaned on its base and paused for a second before toppling over.

About the same time, the three wise men gained their total freedom of movement. They turned to each other with urgency in their faces. "How are we going to get out of here?"

At that moment, the Hindu statue fell against another statue, which fell into a large, skinny vase, which fell into yet another object. Down the objects went like a row of dominoes, until they reached the wall at the end of the window ledge. Leaning against the inside of that wall was a long-handled replica of a medieval battle pike, with what looked like a small ax at the top. The six-foot pike handle wobbled slightly, and then fell straight into the large display window. The window came crashing down, showering splinters and shards of glass everywhere.

"Good job, Thunder!" yelled Chip. They wasted no time jumping out of the window onto the sidewalk and running after Thunder, who was already hot on JW's trail.

Chapter Fifteen

THE BATTLE

Thunder was moving faster than the wise men, creating a large gap between them as they all ran down the sidewalk. Thunder came to a street corner and stopped. He sniffed the air to the left and then to the right. He put his nose back to the ground and started sniffing around in circles. Chip, Harold, and Uncle caught up with Thunder.

"Which way did he go?" Chip asked, breathing hard.

Thunder circled in an ever-widening arc, stopped, and then pointed his nose just like a bird dog—then off he ran again with the wise men barely keeping chase.

This same scene repeated itself two more times. Thunder turned to the left and then to the right. The next street had fewer streetlights. It was darker here, and the shadows stretched longer. Thunder slowed and sniffed more intently. He stopped midway down the street and looked around in confusion. The wise men caught up again. "Are we close?"

"What is it, Thunder?"

"Which way do we go now?"

To their right was a dark, narrow alley that was cluttered with trash-cans, empty boxes, and other debris. As they panted and talked, they did not notice a dark figure rising to its feet from the alley and moving toward them, slowly and quietly.

Thunder was the first to notice the figure closing in on them, and he let out a loud warning grunt as he pointed his nose at the intruder who was now just a few feet away, moving toward them out of the shadows.

The three wise men turned quickly. They froze, terrified, and braced for the worst.

"Well, hi there, little fellas!" came a familiar voice. "Ol' Charlie sure didn't expect to see you's out here tonight."

Chip, Harold, and Uncle let out a deep sigh of relief.

"I was a-plannin' on gettin' in line at the shelter tonight, but I had this strange feeling from the Lord that he wanted me to sit right here in this alley. I wasn't for sure why in the world the Lord would want me sittin' in this here alley, but now I's thinkin' maybe it's got something to do with you little fellas."

The minds of the three wise men had been racing in a near panic when they had turned down this dark street, and they had almost jumped out of their skins when they turned and saw the figure of a man standing right behind them. But hearing Charlie's voice, and hearing him speak of the Lord, made them realize that they had been so frantic and busy chasing after JW that they hadn't allowed time for God to guide their steps.

Chip was the first to speak.

"Charlie, could you actually hear us when we were at the homeless shelter?"

Charlie smiled big. "Well yes, I's sure could! But I's think you was the only one who really spoke to me, Chip." Charlie chuckled and added, "Well, you and dat camel there. I's hasn't been formally introduced to these other two fellas."

Harold and Uncle introduced themselves, and Charlie explained that when he had felt the Lord wanting him to sit in the alley, he had faithfully done just that. He had been waiting for hours to see why the Lord had asked him to do such a strange thing.

After hearing this, the wise men knew for certain that God had sent Charlie to help them. They explained the situation with JW as quickly as they could and told Charlie about the demons.

Charlie listened intently to the whole story and spoke when they were finished.

"Um-hmm, now I *knows* why the Lord wanted me sittin' here in this alley, and I's understands what you's saying about those crafty demon creatures. I's can see them too, yes sir. I's been able to see them alls my life."

"No other people seem to be able to see them," said Chip.

"Well, my little friend, I's reckon most peoples can't. And well, for those who can see them, it makes it mighty rough on a person."

Charlie went back into the alley and grabbed his green duffel bag. He brought it out and sat it down by the wise men.

"I's figure you all can sit on this here knapsack, and I can carry you all. I think Ol' Charlie's legs will carry you faster than your little legs. But before we's get started on any quest or mission for the Lord, the first thing we's got to do is pray and ask the Lord for his providence." Charlie nodded, bowed his head, and led them in a prayer. He asked for JW's protection and for God to use them according to his will.

"Amen," Charlie finished. He looked up and said, "Our prayers will catch up to JW before we does."

The wise men looked at each other, humbled. They had been afraid of what they would be able do when they did catch up to JW, and they still weren't sure how they would face the demons and help their friend, but Charlie, unlikely warrior that he was, had reminded them of one of the most important truths from the Word of God: "All things are possible through Christ who strengthens me."

Charlie slung the strap over one shoulder and carried the bag under his arm at his left side. The three wise men were perched on top, holding on to Charlie's coat as well as the straps of the duffel bag. Thunder continued to run ahead of them on foot. He had no trouble in keeping at Charlie's pace.

Thunder had lost JW's trail, so now, with Charlie's help, they roamed the streets, parks, and alleys, searching for clues that would lead them to their young friend. Charlie talked to other homeless people and asked them if they had seen anyone matching JW's description. No one seemed to notice the wise men clinging to the top of Charlie's bag, and the one person who saw Thunder thought he was a strange-looking squirrel. Most of the homeless people were nice to Charlie, but many of them talked to him as if he were a child, or as if they did not take him very seriously. Some people outright mocked Charlie, laughed at him, and said things like, "Here comes Crazy Charlie!" when they saw him approaching. Charlie seemed not to notice these comments, or else he simply ignored them. He was intent in his efforts to help the wise men and did not let anyone distract him from his mission.

As they searched the streets, Charlie and the wise men got better acquainted.

"You said it's rough on a person when they can see demons. What did you mean by that?" Harold asked Charlie.

"Well, it's pretty much like this. When you sees those sorts of things, they scare you and bother you, especially when you is a child. So you tells people what you sees. People don't like to hear that kind of talk. It's easier for them to just calls you crazy than it is for them to believe what you's saying. It's easier for most folks to just say Ol' Charlie has schiz-o-phrenia or calls him crazy than to believe that he can sees spirits."

"I see how that could be rough," said Harold.

Charlie reflected a bit. "When I was young, I started thinkin' maybe I *is* crazy. If I is the only one who can sees these things, then maybe there is something wrong with me. I's think for a time I was crazy—I couldn't tell what was real and what was not. But you see, I had not given myself to the Lord back in those days. I was angry and scared all the time, in and out of hospitals and sanitariums. They puts me on this drug and that drug—I talked to doctor after doctor. I's even had this doctor who hooked Ol' Charlie up to electrodes and tried to shocks the craziness out of me. I had no hope. That's when the demons started talkin' directly to me. All my life I had seen them at different times, but they's never seemed to pay me any attention. I didn't knows if they even knew I could see them. But I know now that is just part of the game they plays with you."

"What do you mean by 'game'?" Chip asked.

"You see, they wants you to think that you is crazy." Charlie cleared his throat and swallowed hard. "But when you is at your lowest, when you is scared and has lost hope…you see, that is when they takes an interest in you. They told me all sorts of things. I started to believe that I was better off dead."

"What did you do then?" asked Uncle.

"Well, lookin' back now, I's realizes something. When you is at your lowest, that is when the demons take an interest in you—yes—yes, that is true. But what I didn't realize at the time is that is also when the Lord takes a strong interest in you too. Don't gets me wrong—I knows now that the Lord had an interest in me all along, but you sees, I was good at ignoring the Lord just like the demons were good at ignoring me all those years. The Lord had reached out to me, given me plenty of signs all of those years, but I didn't want to believe in God any mores than I wanted to believe in those bad things I could see. I was too interested in doing whats made Charlie happy. I believed that being happy was the most important thing in life. I was always told to 'Believe in yourself, Charlie.' 'You can be whatever you want to be, Charlie.' 'Just has faith in yourself, Charlie.'"

Charlie paused in a moment of deep reflection and said, "A man who just has faith in himself—he doesn't really have no faith at all."

His voice pepped up as he continued talking. "The Lord cured me of that sort of thinkin', though. When you believes in Jesus, you knows the truth, and the truth will set you free. I may has something wrong with my mind; I's may be homeless, and I may get confused sometimes, but I knows that God is with me and has a plan for me. No one can takes that away from me."

Hours had passed by this time, and though it was still dark and cold, the wise men knew it wouldn't be too long before the sun came up.

Charlie pointed at Thunder. "He's on to something."

Sure enough, Thunder's body language changed as he picked up a smell on the sidewalk. They all followed as he headed down the sloping walk and kept in pursuit of the scent for several turns.

Charlie shook his head back and forth and said, "Umm, umm, umm, I's got a bad feeling about this. He's headed down to the Cumberland—down to the river."

As they crisscrossed back and forth, moving steadily on a downhill grade, they started to hear the gentle flow of water. Thunder stopped in the middle of a sidewalk and peered into the darkness of yet another wooded park. All the hair on Thunder's back stood on end as his nose pointed into the darkness.

Charlie quietly came to a stop, got down on one knee, and gently lowered the bag to the ground. In a hushed tone, he said, "I can feel the presence of evil—they is close by."

The wise men slid off the duffel bag and peered into the darkness alongside Charlie and Thunder. They looked down a dirt path beyond some bushes and into a grove of sprawling trees that shadowed a park bench. There, they could see the figure of a young man standing behind the bench, leaning over with both hands on the backrest and his head hung low.

Charlie set his other knee on the ground and whispered to the wise men, "I's got you covered—you's all go and help your friend." Charlie then closed his eyes, clasped his hands, and began whispering intent prayers to God.

Thunder and the wise men carefully crept closer to the man leaning against the bench. Thunder silently moved off to the side while the wise men kept moving together. They paced into the shadows silently and alertly until they were close enough to see that it was indeed JW—and he didn't look good. His face was pale, and he looked confused and disoriented. They could hear the tormenting, hissing voice of the captain and the echo of his band of demons. Their voices were rhythmic and trancelike. They were speaking thoughts into JW's mind.

"Just keep walking…the river is nice, it is fresh and good."

"Yes, yes the water is fine, go and see it, touch it, it will help your pain go away."

"This life is too hard, just let go…it's not worth the pain…wade into the river; let it numb your pain…it will be fine, you will see."

Their urging was intense—but something in JW was resisting. He was fighting, battling with the negative thoughts that were flooding his mind.

JW's mind was fuzzy and swimming with conflicting thoughts. He wasn't sure why he felt the way he did—he was too confused to realize that someone had spiked his drink at Mike's house. The dizziness was worse than ever, and now he was confused as to which way to go to get back home. He just wanted to crawl into bed. But then he thought—*I don't have a bed. I don't really have a home anymore.* Images of his parents' love and their tragic deaths in that car crash haunted him again. He felt the pain in his heart and in his stomach. It was all so unfair. If there really was a God, why did he allow all of these bad things to happen? Other thoughts weaved into his head. *I should keep moving…I should go down to the river…just take a look…maybe get my feet wet or splash some water on my face…maybe I should just jump off a bridge…*

"No!" JW shouted.

He brought his hands to his face, rubbed his eyes, and smacked his cheeks. "What's wrong with me!"

A voice startled JW. He blinked his eyes and quickly wiped his tears on his sleeve.

"Who's there? What do you want?" JW demanded.

The voice came out of the darkness, but JW could see no one.

"It's Harold," the voice said again. "Do you remember me, JW?"

JW eyes peered into the darkness. "Who are you? How do you know my name?"

He backed away from the bench, searching the shadows. Confusing, fearful thoughts flooded his head.

"Harold, Chip, and Uncle...remember us? From the orphanage," the voice said with patience and concern.

A movement on the ground caught JW's eye. He strained to make out what it was. Then, in a patch of moonlight, he saw what looked like three remote-controlled GI Joes walking slowly toward him. No, it was the three wise men from the store window—the same ones from his childhood dream! JW smiled and walked cautiously toward them. Seeing them somehow warmed his heart. But just as quickly as the warm feeling came, he was hit with a troubling thought. A whole torrent of thoughts came flooding into his head. *I must really be losing it...I'm hallucinating...I need to keep moving...moving, yes...I need to go to the river. I need to get out of here.*

"JW!" shouted the voice from the ground again, this time with a sense of urgency. He focused his eyes on the patch of moonlight again. "Listen to us carefully: *don't* listen to those voices inside your head! Focus on us. Listen to us, JW. We are here to help you."

JW was becoming more confused. He now realized that he was hearing three voices. The three distinct voices of the little wise men he had such fond memories of.

"What do you mean, the voices in my head? I—I don't understand."

"God has sent us to help you," Uncle said. "Your mind is playing tricks on you right now. Just stop and ask God to help you. Call out to him—speak his name." The three wise men sounded so clear, so sure.

Negative thoughts flooded through JW's mind again. He questioned his own sanity. Chills washed over him. He felt dread and fear, and yet—and yet—why hadn't he thought of that before? Why wasn't he asking God to help him? He felt the fear in his heart quickly turn to anger. *That's strange,* JW thought in a brief moment of clarity. *Where's that anger coming from?* In a flash, he realized that the wise men were right. Something was going on in his head that wasn't just him. JW pressed his eyes closed and softly murmured, "Jesus, help me."

At that very moment, a cold, eerie breeze brushed past him, and leaves blew in the wind, swirling around where the three little wise men were standing. The wise men looked scared, and each of them moved around as if watching some unseen force that was causing the leaves and dust to pick up around them. JW's dizziness returned, and the world felt like it was moving in circles. He took a few steps and grabbed hold of the park bench again to stabilize himself.

The wise men had said the right things. As soon as JW asked Jesus to help him, the demons angrily turned their attention to the meddling little men.

Bone-chilling screams and hisses shrieked from the mass of wicked fiends as they rushed to encircle the three wise men.

The captain's voice was no longer filled with indifferent mockery as it had been at the Lion's Den; now it was a full-blown, gravelly scream of irrational, bloodthirsty anger.

"How dare you come here to interfere with our work!" sounded the loud voice that penetrated right through the wise men. "You know not the power which you have awakened on this day, little statues of men!" The voice swirled around the three wise men in a fury of motion.

The voices clamored together. "We shall destroy you for interfering with our work, which we have every right in our own eyes to be doing!"

The three wise men stood paralyzed in the middle of a swirl of ravenous, black-hearted beings who buzzed about like a swarm of killer bees.

Meanwhile, Charlie's prayers increased in urgency and fervency. "O Lord, to you be the power and the glory! I's pray that you would protect these little servants of yours and this young man, JW. I pray in Jesus' name that you would build a hedge of protection around them and send your angels to protect them…"

All the while, Thunder had gone unnoticed by the demons. He was observing everything from the shadows of a nearby bush. Sensing that his comrades were in trouble, he burst from the bush with a loud, squealing, high-pitched grunt. Thunder barreled right through the demons into his three friends and knocked them all two feet back and away from the encircling mass of death. The three wise men, along with Thunder, tumbled and rolled, and then instinctively hopped back to their feet and formed into a line, standing shoulder to shoulder with one another. As they did, they let out a loud, "Hee-ya!" just as they had seen students

do in Pastor Jones's karate class. Each of the wise men looked at one another as if to say, *Why did we just do that?*

To their surprise, the demons stopped and didn't attack. Instead, the foggy mass transformed, separated, and materialized into the forms of thirteen large men with wings, holding dull, gray, lackluster swords. They did not radiate or gleam; they were dreary, drab creatures with sunken, dark eyes. They had pasty-looking skin and distorted faces that looked anything but human. Then, something even more surprising happened. The demons held their swords defensively and moved backward. After a few steps, they looked cautiously from side to side as if they really had something to be concerned about. The wise men were confused—surely, the demons were not that easy to bluff?

It was only then that the wise men noticed the light shining from behind their position. They all turned their heads slowly. There, standing right behind them, was the angel from Clemons's Store. His face was expressionless except for his shining eyes, which were intently narrowed and focused directly at the Commander and his small horde. The wise men had never felt so relieved in their entire existence as they did at that very moment.

At the same time, JW was still dealing with a rush of confusing thoughts and a fuzzy mind. He could not see all that was going on in the spiritual realm, but he could feel it. The forces of good and the forces of evil were all around him. JW did not understand what was happening; he just knew he had to get out of the area as quickly as he could. He stumbled and ran up the dirt path, catching himself against trees as he moved. He reached the street and supported himself on a guardrail for a moment, then headed up the sidewalk. The horizon was beginning to glow with the dark orange color of predawn.

The angel spoke. "Little ones, you go after JW—I will handle *them*." Smoothly and effortlessly, he pulled out his large, gleaming sword while keeping his eyes focused intently on the demons.

The wise men and Thunder raced after JW. As they moved away, they could hear battle cries and the thunderous clanging of swords behind them. The air had the feel of supernatural electricity running through it, making hairs stand on end and leaving a prickly sensation on the skin. The sky growled with thunder deep in its throat.

In the streets, cars were passing at a regular pace as the city came to life for another busy workday. Trash trucks moved in the alleyways, picking up dumpsters and banging them into their bellies before setting them down. A street sweeper with its rotating brushes moved slowly along, cleaning the gutter.

"There he is!" said Uncle, looking up the street as they came off the dirt path.

JW had paused, leaning against a large public trash bin. He was still trying to clear his head. His heart was pumping quickly, and he was confused and scared.

"JW! Wait, let us help you!" the wise men called as they ran after him.

JW heard their faint calls and turned to see them running up the street. Still convinced that he was hallucinating, JW said, "No, leave me alone!" He turned and bolted into the street.

The sickening sound of screeching tires filled the air, followed by a dull thud.

JW had run right in front of an oncoming car. The driver hit the brakes and came to a stop, but not before hitting JW. He was knocked several feet and tumbled to a limp, unconscious heap in the middle of the street.

"JW!" yelled the wise men in horror.

They ran toward JW, but just as they hopped off the sidewalk, the first rays of early morning sun filtered through the trees and between the buildings.

Sirens blared in the distance and came closer and closer before stopping when they were at their loudest. Charlie was still kneeling in the grass, rocking back and forth with his eyes closed, deep in prayer, when a hand gently reached down and touched his shoulder. Charlie slowly opened his eyes and looked up to see an angel of the Lord standing above him.

The angel said, "Thank you for your help, my friend. The battle is over now. May the Lord be with you always."

Charlie simply smiled and said, "You's welcome."

The angel vanished in a flash of light.

When Charlie stood up, he saw the blinking lights of the ambulance and police cars. An officer was directing traffic while another was talking to a frantic woman who was saying, "He just ran out in front of me. I didn't have time to stop!"

Charlie stood and watched the paramedics carefully transferring JW onto a gurney and placing him in the back of the ambulance.

As Charlie watched, his eyes lowered to the gutter in front of him. There were the wise men and the camel, back in their ceramic form.

Charlie picked them up and carefully placed them in his duffel bag. Then he headed up the street.

Chapter Sixteen

HOME

The smell of musty cardboard filled the air, permeated by the distant scratching of a mouse.

"Well, here we are again. Still in the dark," Harold said plainly.

"How many Christmases has it been now?" asked Chip.

"I think this is number five since we last saw JW lying in the street—five years trapped in this dark, quiet box," Uncle stated. He sighed.

Indeed, it had been five years since the battle in the park. The wise men came to life each year just like always, but they were stuck away somewhere in a dark box, crowded and packed together with a bunch of other unseen objects. They had tried each year to free themselves, with no success. Each year, their conversations ranged from encouraging each other to keep faith and hope, to pondering whether God had forgotten about them, or worse—wondering if this was their punishment for not saving JW in time. But they rarely allowed themselves to dwell on the negative. "We have been down that road before," they reasoned.

They discussed why it was always so easy and tempting to assume God was angry with them or punishing them when they simply didn't like or understand their circumstances. But they had grown too much and seen too much to allow those negative thoughts to take them captive. After all, hadn't God brought them around the world and back into JW's life? Hadn't God trained them through their circumstances and taught them through the people he had brought into their lives? Hadn't God sent Ol' Charlie when they were lost and the angel when they needed protection? Yes, they were now in the dark. Stuck in a situation that was out of their control to change. They did not like or understand their circumstances. All this was true—but in spite of it, they resolved that they would not allow themselves to fall into despair, no matter how tempting and easy it might be to do so.

Days passed.

"Hey, I can move again! Uh, well, sort of. It's still cramped in here," said Chip.

"Let's sing some Christmas carols and hymns," Harold suggested.

"Great idea!" they all agreed, and into the early morning, they sang.

Another year went by. Another December 12th arrived.

"Hello? Are you all still here?"

Two yeses and a grunt answered Chip.

"It appears we are still stuffed in a dark box somewhere. So is this Christmas number six?"

"Yes, it is," came the answer.

Time passed.

"Did you hear that?" Chip whispered.

"Yeah."

"Yes."

"Grumpf."

There was a sound—they could hear movement, rustling, and voices!

It wasn't long after hearing the noises and the muffled sound of voices that the wise men got to see light again as they were unpacked by some women and set on a table in a room with lots of other tables. All the tables were covered with knickknacks, arts and crafts, and baked goods. On the walls were various religious decorations, including a cross and pictures of biblical scenes.

A large poster on a bulletin board across the room read:

The Church Christmas Bazaar: December 14–16

Women with aprons carried baked goods from behind a swinging door and placed them on tables. An elderly gentleman stuck his finger in some cinnamon-roll icing and brought it to his mouth when no one was looking, while another man filled his Styrofoam cup with coffee. At exactly 8:00 a.m., people started filing into the room from an outside door. They browsed and exchanged money for the treasures they found atop the tables. The wise men were so happy to once again see people and watch them interact and come and go.

There was another rush of people at 10 a.m.; mostly women, some with children in tow. They browsed, talked, and laughed. They ate the homemade cinnamon rolls, drank coffee and juice, and all the while bought things from the mass of items spread upon numerous tables.

No one seemed too interested in the wise men figurines. They were a little dinged up, and as was the story of their lives, they didn't really match any Nativity set that anyone owned. The rush died down and then picked up again around lunchtime. A woman named Barbara was working behind the table where the wise men were on display.

"Hello, Barbara! How are you today?" asked a young woman who walked up to their table. In her early twenties, she had shoulder-length blonde hair and blue eyes that smiled as easily as her lips. She was fit, with an athletic build that went naturally with the sweatpants and tennis shoes she was wearing.

"Oh, hi!" Barbara replied. "How's the new mom-to-be doing?"

"Oh, I am doing great," the young woman said with a smile. "A little morning sickness, but it hasn't been too bad yet."

"If you need help with anything, you just let me know. I remember how excited and scared I was with my first child. So even if you just want someone to talk to, I would be happy to be there for you."

The young woman smiled again, her blue eyes warm and genuinely grateful. "Thank you so much, Barbara. Everyone here at the church has been so nice to us since we moved into town."

The young woman placed her hands across her rounded abdomen. "I really need to do some shopping; I can't just wear sweatpants for the rest of my pregnancy."

Barbara chuckled. "I suppose not. Hey, I hear that your hubby found a job. That didn't take too long. What is he going to be doing?"

"Well, you know I'm a little biased, but any employer would be crazy not to hire such a great guy." She smiled proudly. "He'll be working with kids at a twenty-four-hour shelter for runaway and homeless youth."

Barbara gasped. "Oh my, that sounds interesting. Do we really have that many runaway and homeless kids here in Nebraska? I mean, can this size of a community sustain something like that?"

"You would be surprised just how big the need really is," the young woman replied as her eyes fell upon the wise men.

"Oh, look at these!" She picked up Harold to inspect him. "Wow, these are really nice. I was kind of hoping I would find some decorations for our new home." She set Harold down and picked up Chip and Thunder. "This camel is so cute! How much are these? I have to have them."

Barbara smiled. "You should see your face—all lit up like a kid on Christmas morning. I didn't realize those ceramic wise men were so special. Tell you what. Why don't you let me treat you to them as a housewarming gift?"

"Oh, that's not necessary," the young woman answered.

"No, no, I insist. Here, I'll wrap them up for you. I really want to do this for you."

The young woman broke into her beautiful smile again. "Thank you so much, Barbara."

"It looks like we are going to a new home!" Harold said happily.

"She seems nice, and she thinks you're cute, Thunder, did you hear that?" Chip said.

Thunder grunted a happy grunt.

When she got home, the young woman set the wise men up as the centerpiece on the kitchen table in the small home she and her husband shared. The kitchen and dining room were one space with a stove, sink, refrigerator, and a few cabinets occupying half of the room. The other side of the room was just big enough to fit four or five people around the small dining room table. The open doorway that led to the living room parted the space. It was an old house with dated appliances and a hodgepodge of yard-sale furniture, but it was neat and tidy.

Later that evening, the young woman was preparing dinner when they all heard the sound of an automobile pulling up outside of the house. She peeked through the curtains, smiled, and went through the kitchen doorway into the living room. The wise men heard a door open and close. Voices drifted back to the kitchen.

"Hi, sweetie! How was work today?"

"Hey, it was great! I really like my job—I just love working with the kids. I think I'm going to be able to make a difference there. Mmm, something smells good!"

"I'm cooking spaghetti."

There was a moment of quiet followed by laughter. "Okay, what are you smiling about? You know you can't hide anything from me," the young woman's husband said.

"Well, I went to the church bazaar today, and I picked up a little surprise for you while I was there."

"Cinnamon rolls?"

"No," she said, laughing, "something a little more special than that. You know the story you told me the other night? Well, it's so weird—I was just standing there talking to Barbara, and all of a sudden, I looked down, and there they were."

"There *who* were? You didn't bring home a kitten, did you?"

"No! Well, just come to the kitchen and see. Wait…close your eyes and take my hand. No peeking!"

There was more laughter as the young woman's voice grew louder.

"Watch out—turn this way, around the couch…okay, keep coming."

The young couple came into the kitchen.

"Open your eyes!"

The young man looked around, smiling, and then saw the wise men on the table. The smile left his face, and his mouth slowly fell open as he walked to the table. He knelt down and just stared at the little ceramic statues.

A worried look came over the young woman's face.

"JW, you do like them, don't you?"

JW reached over and picked up Chip and Thunder. His fingers gently rubbed over the broken chip on the ceramic robe.

"I thought they looked just like the ones you described in your story. You do like them?"

JW turned around, tears streaking down his face. "Sweetheart, I think these *are* the ones from my story—I absolutely love them!"

JW stood and embraced his wife for a long moment.

In the silence, a tiny *sniff, sniff* could be heard.

Harold inquired, "Chip, are you crying?"

"Yes, Harold, my heart is crying tears of joy," said Chip.

"Me too," Harold confessed. "Me too."

"We are home," Uncle added. "We are finally home."

Epilogue

"What did you say the camel's name is?" JW's wife asked as she rolled a forkful of spaghetti.

"Thunder," JW answered.

"Hmm, that's really weird," she said.

"Yeah, it's kind of a strange name for a camel," JW answered with a smile.

"No, it's not that—I just remembered something from when I was a little girl."

She smiled as she closed her eyes and recited her favorite Bible verse: "Do not forget to entertain strangers, for by so doing some people have entertained angels without knowing it."

"Hebrews 13:2," JW said. "That's the Bible verse on the plaque you have hanging in the living room, isn't it, Abby?"

Abigail's face brightened as memories entered her mind. "Yeah, it's the second verse I memorized as a child—the first one was John 3:16. I haven't thought about this for a long time, but when I was a little girl—I think I was maybe five years old—I was at the hospital with my mom and grandma because my grandpa was having surgery. I remember I was lying on a couch in the waiting room when I saw something move across the room…"

Following a long line of slow-moving passengers, Hector Boa boarded the plane, looking at his boarding pass to double-check his seat number.

This will be a long flight to London. I hope I don't sit next to some moron who wants to jibber-jabber for twelve hours, Hector thought to himself. The flight was the price Hector paid to take an annual trip to Europe to hunt for antiques and exotic collectables, both for his personal collection and to sell in his Lion's Den store in Nashville.

Hector found his seat, stowed his small bag in one of the overhead compartments, and sat down. He looked at face after face of the people shuffling up the aisle of the airplane, watching their eyes for a hint that they might be looking for the numbers above his seat. Hector was already in a bad mood just imagining all of the annoying people and personalities that could be stuck next to him on this already too-long international flight.

Hector had just managed to lose himself in thought when a polite gentleman with a British accent said, "Excuse me, sir, may I get in? I'm in the seat next to you."

The first thing Hector noticed when he looked up was a silver cross hanging on a chain around the man's neck.

As Hector faked a smile and rose to let the man in, he thought, *Oh great! I hope he's not some religious nut who feels it's his duty in life to save my eternal soul from damnation. Religious freaks! They're the worst!*

Hector settled back into his aisle seat and turned a shoulder away from the man, hoping he would get the hint that he wasn't in the mood to talk.

"So what are you going to London for?" the man asked, leaning forward to get Hector's attention.

Annoyed, Hector replied with a one-word answer.

"Business."

"I'm headed back home," the man said. "I work as a marketing consultant for nonprofit organizations, orphanages, Christian ministries, and the like."

Hector grunted in uninterested acknowledgment.

The man didn't get the hint. "So what type of business are you in, if you don't mind my asking?"

A thought went through Hector's mind: *Yes, I do mind you asking. Now why don't you shut up and read a book or something?*

But Hector really didn't like conflict, and after all, he could get out of talking easily enough when the plane took off. He could just close his eyes and pretend to be asleep. He thought about doing that now, but the man was still waiting patiently.

"Antiques; I deal in antiques," he finally answered.

"Oh, very good, very good," answered the stranger. "I used to have quite the eye for antiques myself. Only the best, though, only the rarest, the most expensive, the most unique items…anything that would bring the highest price. That's what used to interest me."

Now Hector was really annoyed. It was bad enough that this total stranger was trying to strike up a conversation with him, but now the man had gone and peaked Hector's interest. He would probably regret it, but he just had to ask.

"What do you mean by '*used to* interest me'?

"Well, to put it bluntly, I was a thief," the man said with a smile. "I would steal antiques and sell them to buyers on the black market."

Hector shifted in his seat to face the man. On second thought, this guy might have some interesting stories to tell. Stealing things to sell on the black market—now that was the type of thing Hector might enjoy talking about.

"So tell me about some of the things you *used to* steal," Hector said with a devious grin.

The stranger held out his hand. "It's nice to meet you…"

"I'm Hector."

They shook hands.

The man settled back into his seat as though he was priming himself for a long story. "My name is Nick," he began.

To find out what happened at the factory and why Mr. Clemons never got his Nativity set, go to the official *Wee Three Kings* website for one final epilogue.

www.WeeThreeKings.com

About The Author

Brent L. Anderson lives in the wide open spaces of Wyoming with his beautiful wife and three creative children. He is the full time Executive Director of a non-profit organization, a martial arts instructor, a small business owner, an inventor, and a writer of books in his spare time.

Made in the USA
San Bernardino, CA
29 September 2015